The Garden of the Fall

Regina Bergen

Dedication

For Eve.

For Leora.

For Liora.

The women who chose.

CHAPTER ONE

The Garden That Never Changes

Leora woke to birdsong—the same three-note trill that had greeted her every morning for as long as she could remember. She stretched, her fingers reaching toward dappled sunlight that fell through leaves in patterns she knew by heart. The moss beneath her was soft and dry, warmed by the sun to exactly the temperature her body preferred. Perfect, as always.

She sat up slowly, pushing dark hair from her face, and looked around at the glade where she'd spent the night. Morning glories climbed the nearby oak in a spiral so precise it could have been measured. Dew drops clung to spider webs, each one catching light like a jewel deliberately placed. Even the air smelled orchestrated—honeysuckle and fresh grass, with just a hint of the wild roses that grew in careful clusters along the forest edge.

Leora's stomach made a soft sound, and as if on cue, she noticed the berry bushes to her left had ripened overnight. Fat blackberries hung heavy on their branches, perfectly ripe, waiting. She plucked one and brought it to her lips, the juice staining her fingertips purple. Sweet. Of course it was sweet. It was always sweet, always ripe at exactly the moment she needed it.

She ate mechanically, one berry after another, until her hunger faded. Then she stood and brushed moss from her bare legs, wincing slightly at a chill that seemed to come from inside her rather than from the mild morning air.

The sensation had started recently—or perhaps not recently at all. Time moved strangely here. Days blurred into weeks into seasons that never actually changed, only existed in different places. She could walk from spring to winter in an afternoon, from summer to fall in an hour. But nothing ever *transitioned*. Spring remained eternally spring in its designated quadrant of the forest, and fall stayed fall in its corner, and they never touched, never bled into one another the way she sometimes thought they should.

Leora walked toward the sound of running water, her feet finding the path without conscious thought. She'd walked this way a thousand times—or was it ten thousand? She couldn't remember. The circular stone wall that contained the spring-fed pool appeared through the trees, exactly where it always was, and she knelt beside it, cupping her hands to drink.

The water was ice-cold and crystalline, just as perfect as everything else. She could see every pebble at the bottom of the pool, every ripple her hands made spreading outward in mathematically precise circles.

"Is there anything beyond the trees?" she asked the water, her voice barely a whisper.

The pool didn't answer. It never did. But something else might have—that presence she'd felt her entire life, the hum beneath everything, the invisible force that kept the fruit ripe, the paths clear, and the seasons locked in place. She'd never seen it, never heard it speak directly, but she knew it was there. Watching. Tending. Maintaining.

Keeping her safe.

Keeping her alone.

Leora shook her head sharply, as if she could dislodge the thought before it took root. She wasn't supposed to think like that. Safety was good. Solitude was peace. The Garden provided everything she could possibly need. What more could there be?

But the chill in her chest deepened, spreading through her ribs like frost on a window.

She stood abruptly and set off walking, not toward anywhere in particular, just away. Her bare feet moved silently over earth that seemed to soften wherever she stepped, paths that appeared just when she needed them. The trees parted for her. The underbrush never caught her skin. Even the sunlight seemed to follow her, ensuring she was never in shadow unless she wanted to be.

By midday—or what she thought was midday, though the sun never seemed to move quite right—she found herself at the border between spring and summer. On her left, apple blossoms hung eternally on the verge of blooming. On her right, fruit trees drooped with the weight of ripe peaches and plums that would never fall, never rot, never do anything but wait.

Leora reached out and touched the invisible line between them. The air was warmer on the summer side, cooler on the spring side, but the transition was so abrupt it felt wrong. Unnatural. Like someone had drawn a line and said, "This is where spring ends," without asking spring if it wanted to linger, to gradually warm, to slowly transform into something else.

"Don't you want to change?" she whispered to the apple tree.

Its blossoms trembled slightly in a breeze that felt, for just a moment, like an answer.

She pulled her hand back, heart racing for no reason she could name.

This was the problem with the questions. Once they started, they didn't stop. They piled up in her mind like fallen leaves that no invisible force came to sweep away. Questions about the borders between seasons, about why she was alone, about whether anything existed beyond the forest, about time and change and what it meant to live in a place where nothing ever ended because nothing ever really began.

Leora pressed her palm against her chest, feeling her heartbeat, trying to anchor herself in something real and undeniable. She existed. She breathed. She felt things—hunger and satisfaction, warmth and that strange new cold that had nothing to do with temperature.

She existed, but sometimes she wondered if she was truly alive.

The thought made her gasp aloud, and she clapped a hand over her mouth as if she could take it back. No. That was too much. Too dangerous. The questions needed to stop before they took her somewhere she couldn't return from.

She turned away from the border and walked deeper into summer, letting the heat chase away her doubts. She picked an apricot from a low-hanging branch and bit into it, the sweetness flooding her mouth. She found a patch of clover and lay down in it, staring up at a sky so perfectly blue it looked painted.

The chill in her chest did not fade.

As the sun began its lazy descent—slower here than in other parts of the Garden, she'd noticed—Leora made her way north. She walked faster now, with purpose, her feet carrying her along paths she'd traveled more and more frequently in recent days. Or weeks. Or however long it had been since she'd first felt the pull.

The air grew crisp as she entered the autumn zone. Leaves crunched beneath her feet—orange and gold and deep crimson, perpetually falling from trees that, somehow, never grew bare. The scent changed too: woodsmoke and overripe apples, cinnamon and decay. Not the sterile perfection of the other gardens, but something wilder. Something that smelled like possibility.

Leora's pulse quickened as she spotted the gate.

It rose from the ground like something that had grown there rather than been built, iron and vine twisted together into an arch. Rust ate at the metal in places, and the carvings that might have once been ornate had softened with time and neglect. Unlike everything else in the Garden, this gate looked old. Used. Forgotten.

Beyond it lay the Garden of the Fall.

She'd discovered it by accident—or perhaps by design—several weeks ago. Since then, she'd returned repeatedly, drawn by something she couldn't name. The Garden of the Fall was different from the other seasonal zones. Where spring was eternally budding and summer eternally lush and winter eternally dormant, fall was perpetually letting go. Leaves fell and fell and fell, never accumulating into an unmanageable pile but never stopping their descent either. Fruit hung overripe on the trees, bruised and sweet and just on the verge of rot.

It was the only place in the Garden that felt like it was at least moving toward something, even if that something was an ending.

Leora pushed the gate, and it swung open with a groan that echoed in a way sound never did in the other gardens. She stepped through, and immediately the air changed. Thicker. Warmer. Almost humid, carrying scents that were too strong, too real: fermented apples and fungal spores and the loamy richness of soil that was actually decomposing, actually feeding new growth.

Her skin prickled with something that might have been warning or might have been anticipation.

The path was overgrown here, roots breaking through the earth as if the ground itself was becoming restless. Trees leaned at angles that suggested they'd never been tended, never been told to grow straight. Vines tangled through branches without care for aesthetics. And everywhere—*everywhere*—leaves spiraled down from above, their descent chaotic and beautiful and nothing like the choreographed perfection of the other gardens.

Leora walked deeper, her breathing shallow, her heart beating faster than usual. She passed gnarled apple trees heavy with fruit that actually looked like it might fall. She stepped over mushroom circles that sprouted from rotting logs. She brushed past wildflowers that grew in clumps rather than careful arrangements.

And then she saw it.

The tree.

It stood in the farthest corner of the Garden of the Fall, massive and impossible and utterly out of place. While everything else in this garden was in the process of letting go, this tree held on. Its leaves were a deep, eternal green—waxy and thick with veins so dark they looked almost black. Where other trees bent and swayed, this one stood perfectly still, as if it existed outside the wind's reach, outside time itself.

Its roots were tremendous, spreading across the ground like searching fingers, diving deep into earth that seemed to pulse faintly beneath Leora's feet. And its fruit...

Leora stopped walking, staring up at the heavy globes that hung from its branches. They were unlike any fruit she'd seen elsewhere in the Garden— as dark as garnets and glossy as glass, somewhere between an apple and a pomegranate in shape. They caught the amber light of the setting sun and seemed to glow from within, and their scent...

She breathed in and felt dizzy.

The fruit smelled oversweet, intoxicating, like honey mixed with wine... and something darker she had no name for. It filled her lungs and made her head feel light, made her body feel heavy, made that chill in her chest spread and shift until it was no longer cold but hot, burning, demanding.

Her fingers itched to reach up and pluck one.

She didn't.

Not yet.

But she knew—had known since the moment she first saw this tree—that eventually she would. That she was meant to. That this tree, unlike everything else in the Garden, was waiting for her to make a choice.

And choice was the one thing the Garden had never asked of her before.

Leora sank down at the base of the tree, nestling between two massive roots, and let out a deep breath. The bark was rough against her back. The ground was bare here. No moss, no grass, nothing that might soften or rot. Just hard-packed earth that seemed to resist even the falling leaves that drifted toward it.

This was where she'd been spending most of her nights lately. She'd gathered dried grass from the summer garden and woven it into a mat, covered it with banana leaves stitched together with thorns and vines. It wasn't as soft as the moss beds the Garden provided elsewhere, but it was hers. She'd made it. She'd chosen it.

The chill—or was it warmth now?—settled deep in her bones as she leaned her head back against the tree and looked up through its branches at the darkening sky.

Somewhere in the Garden, that presence, the Keeper as she'd started calling it in her mind, was watching. She could feel its attention like a weight, like disapproval, like concern.

But here, beneath this tree that didn't belong, that refused to shed or change or obey, Leora felt something else entirely.

She felt awake.

And once you'd felt that, once you'd tasted the difference between existing and truly being alive, there was no going back to sleep.

Even if you wanted to.

Chapter Two

First Touch

Leora woke to the sensation of being watched.

It was different from the Keeper's presence—that constant, invisible attention that felt like being held in place by gentle hands. This was sharper. Closer. Real in a way that made her skin prickle and her breath catch.

She opened her eyes slowly, still nestled between the tree's roots, and saw nothing. Just the garden in early morning light, amber and gold, with mist curling through the falling leaves. The same view she'd woken to for days now.

But the feeling persisted. A pressure at the back of her neck. A certainty that she was not alone.

Leora sat up carefully, pushing tangled hair from her face, and scanned the garden. Her makeshift bed rustled beneath her. The dried grass and banana leaves she'd woven together held their shape through the night. Above, the tree's dark fruit gleamed in the slanted sunlight, and the air was thick with that intoxicating sweetness that made her head swim if she breathed too deeply.

Nothing moved.

She was being ridiculous. She'd been alone her entire life. Why would that change now?

But as she started to stand, brushing leaves from her arms, something shifted in her peripheral vision. A shadow that didn't match the trees. A shape that was too tall, too solid, too—

Human.

Leora's heart lurched into her throat. She spun toward the movement and found herself staring at someone she'd never seen before, someone who shouldn't exist, someone who looked almost like her but profoundly, unmistakably different.

He stood perhaps ten paces away, half-hidden behind the trunk of a smaller tree, and he was staring at her with the same shocked expression she knew must be on her own face.

For a long moment, neither of them moved. Neither of them breathed.

He was taller than her by several inches, his frame broader through the shoulders and chest. Where her body curved, his was all planes and angles. His skin was darker than hers, burnished like wood left in the sun, and his hair was shorter, dark, and slightly wild as if he'd been running his hands through it. His eyes, even from this distance, were startlingly blue—the color of the sky in the spring garden at midday.

And he was looking at her like she was the most impossible thing he'd ever seen.

"You're..." Leora's voice came out barely above a whisper. "You're real?"

He took a step forward, then stopped as if he'd hit an invisible barrier. His hands flexed at his sides. "I—I thought I was the only one."

The words hit her like a physical blow. "So did I."

They stared at each other, and Leora's mind raced to make sense of this. Another person. Someone like her, but not like her. Someone who existed in the same Garden but had somehow remained hidden, separate, unknown. How? Why? Had the Keeper kept them apart deliberately?

The thought sent anger flashing through her chest, hot and unfamiliar.

"How long have you been here?" she asked, taking a step toward him. "In the Garden?"

He shook his head slowly. "I don't... I'm not sure. As long as I can remember? Forever?" His eyes traced her face, her shoulders, her bare arms, as if he was trying to memorize every detail. "I live mostly in the winter garden. And the spring, sometimes. I've never—" He gestured around them at the Garden of the Fall. "I've never come here before. It always felt... forbidden."

"It is," Leora said softly. "Or it's supposed to be, I think. But I can't stay away."

His gaze shifted to the massive tree behind her, and something flickered across his face. Awe, maybe. Or fear. "The tree. I can feel it from here. It's—" He paused, searching for words. "It's calling, isn't it?"

"Yes." The admission felt like a confession. She'd never said it aloud before.

He took another step closer, and Leora could see him more clearly now. The way his chest rose and fell with each breath. The slight tremor in his hands. The pulse beating visibly in his throat. He was nervous, she realized. Just as nervous as she was.

"I'm Leora," she said, the name feeling strange on her tongue. She'd never had reason to introduce herself before. Had never had anyone to speak her name to except the birds and the trees and the silent, watchful Keeper.

"Theren." His voice was deeper than hers, rougher, and hearing it sent a strange shiver down her spine. "I'm Theren."

They stood there, ten paces apart, speaking each other's names silently in their minds as if testing the shape of them.

Then Theren took another step, and another, and Leora found herself moving toward him too, drawn by something she had no words for. Curiosity, yes, but deeper than that. A pull that felt as inevitable as the tree's.

When they were only an arm's length apart, they both stopped.

Up close, Leora could see details she'd missed from a distance. A small scar on his shoulder, pale against his darker skin. The way his eyes weren't just blue but flecked with gray and green, like water reflecting sky and trees. The faint dusting of hair on his forearms that caught the morning light. He smelled different too—not like berries or flowers or any of the orchestrated scents of the Garden, but like sun-warmed skin and something earthier, muskier, entirely his own.

She wanted to reach out and touch him, to confirm he was solid and real, but her hand stayed frozen at her side.

Theren was staring at her just as intently. His gaze moved from her eyes to her hair to her mouth, then lower, and she felt suddenly, strangely aware of her own body in a way she never had been before. The curve of her hips. The rise and fall of her chest with each breath. The way her bare feet were planted in the earth, grounding her.

"You're..." He trailed off, shaking his head slightly. "I don't have words for what you are."

"Neither do I," Leora whispered. "For you."

The air between them seemed to thicken, to hum with the same energy that radiated from the tree. Leora's heart was beating too fast, her skin too warm despite the cool morning air. She wanted to step closer. She wanted to step back. She wanted to understand what this feeling was—this strange mixture of fear and fascination and something else, something that made her want to press her hand to his chest just to feel if his heart was racing like hers.

She reached out.

Her fingertips brushed his forearm—just barely, just a whisper of contact—and the sensation that shot through her was like lightning striking. Not pain, but shock. Heat. A connection that made every nerve in her body light up at once.

Theren gasped, pulling back slightly, his eyes wide. "What was that?"

"I don't know." Leora's hand was shaking. She stared at her own fingers as if they'd betrayed her. "I've never, I mean, nothing's ever felt like that before."

They were both breathing hard now, staring at each other with something that looked almost like panic. But underneath the panic was something else. A hunger. A need to touch again, to understand, to feel that lightning strike twice.

Leora took a breath to speak, to ask him if he felt it too, if he understood any of this better than she did. But the wind picked up suddenly, violently, tearing through the Garden of the Fall with a force that sent leaves swirling in chaotic spirals. The trees groaned, branches creaking, and somewhere in the distance, something that sounded like thunder rumbled even though the sky was clear.

Leora and Theren both froze, looking around.

The air had changed. That gentle, constant warmth that permeated the Garden was gone, replaced by something sharper. Colder. The Keeper's presence, which had always felt like a soft blanket, now felt like a hand pressing down on her chest.

"What's happening?" Theren's voice was tight with alarm.

"I think—" Leora's own voice shook. "I think the Keeper knows. That we've found each other."

As if in answer, a voice echoed through the garden—not spoken aloud but felt in their bones, resonating through the earth and air:

You were not meant to meet. Not yet. Not here.

It wasn't angry, exactly. But it wasn't pleased either. There was something in that voice that reminded Leora of worry, of fear, of a parent catching a child reaching toward a hot flame they'd been warned to stay away from.

Theren moved closer to her instinctively, as if his body knew before his mind did that they needed to stand together against this. His shoulder brushed hers, and even through the fear, Leora felt that same electric awareness, that pull.

"Why not?" she called out to the empty air, her voice stronger than she felt. "Why were we kept separate?"

This place is not for you, the voice continued, and the wind grew stronger, tearing at Leora's hair, making the tree's branches sway even though they'd been still moments before. *Return to your gardens. Forget what you have seen. There is still time to choose peace.*

"No." The word burst from Leora before she could stop it. "I won't forget. I won't pretend I'm alone again."

She turned to Theren, searching his face, terrified he would agree with the Keeper, would walk away, would leave her to this solitude she now knew she couldn't bear.

But Theren was looking at her with something fierce and determined in his eyes. He reached out slowly, deliberately, and took her hand in his. His palm was warm, his fingers strong, and the touch sent that lightning sensation racing up her arm again. But this time she didn't pull away. Neither did he.

"I won't either," he said, his voice steady even though his hand was shaking. "I don't understand what this is, but I won't walk away from it. From you."

The Garden shuddered around them. Flowers that had been blooming began to wilt at the edges. Fruit that had hung heavy on branches tumbled to the ground with soft, bruised thuds. Even the ever-falling leaves seemed to fall faster, more desperately, as if the Garden itself was losing its grip.

Then you choose the path of knowledge, the voice said, and this time there was something that sounded like grief in it. *You choose questions over contentment. Awareness over innocence. This cannot be undone.*

"I know," Leora whispered, gripping Theren's hand tighter.

The wind died as suddenly as it had risen. The Garden fell into an unnatural stillness, and the Keeper's presence receded—not gone, but watching from a distance, waiting.

Leora and Theren stood hand in hand beneath the eternal tree, their fingers intertwined, and the world felt different than it had just minutes before. Bigger. More dangerous. More real.

"What happens now?" Theren asked quietly.

Leora looked up at the tree's dark fruit gleaming above them, then back at Theren's face—this impossible person who'd appeared in her Garden like an answer to a question she'd been too afraid to ask.

"I don't know," she said. "But I think everything just changed."

Theren's thumb traced a slow circle on the back of her hand, and the sensation made her breath catch. He noticed, and something in his expression shifted—surprise giving way to curiosity, to that same hungry awareness she felt burning in her own chest.

"Yes," he said softly. "I think it did."

Above them, the tree's branches rustled in a wind that shouldn't exist, and one of the dark fruits twisted on its stem, catching the light.

Waiting.

Chapter Three

Hunger and Lightning

They didn't let go of each other's hands.

Not when the Garden's unnatural stillness finally broke, and the leaves resumed their endless falling. Not when the sun climbed higher, turning the mist to gold. Not even when a deer emerged from the undergrowth, took one look at them standing there beneath the tree, and bolted as if they'd become something dangerous.

Leora watched the animal flee and felt a pang of loss. The creatures had never feared her before. They'd curled against her on cold nights, eaten from her palms, followed her through the gardens like she was part of their landscape.

"They're afraid of us now," she said quietly.

Theren's grip on her hand tightened slightly. "Or of what we're becoming."

She looked up at him, studying the line of his jaw, the way worry creased the space between his brows. "What are we becoming?"

"I don't know." His thumb was still tracing those slow circles on her hand, and she wondered if he even realized he was doing it. "But I don't think we can stop it. Even if we wanted to."

"Do you want to?" The question came out smaller than she'd intended, vulnerable in a way that made her chest ache. "Want to stop, I mean. Go back to before."

Theren turned to face her fully, and the intensity in his eyes made her breath catch. "Before this morning, I'd spent my entire existence thinking I was alone. That this—" He gestured at the Garden around them with his free hand. "—was all there was. And I was... content, I suppose. I didn't know there was anything to want."

"And now?"

"Now I can't imagine going back to not knowing you exist." His voice dropped lower, rough with emotion. "Even if it means the Garden itself turns against us."

Something warm and bright bloomed in Leora's chest, chasing away the chill that had lived there for so long. She squeezed his hand, marveling at how natural it felt already, how right, even though they'd only just met.

"I feel the same way," she said. "Like I've been asleep my whole life, and you're—" She paused, searching for the right words. "You're what woke me up."

The air between them felt thick again, charged with that same energy that had sparked when they first touched. Theren's gaze dropped to her mouth for just a moment before flicking back to her eyes, and Leora's pulse jumped.

She wanted to close the distance between them. Wanted to learn what his skin felt like beyond just his hand, wanted to press herself against the solid warmth of him and see if that lightning sensation would spread through her entire body.

But fear held her back. Fear of the intensity of it, of how little she understood about what was happening, of the Keeper's warning that still echoed in her bones.

Theren seemed to sense her hesitation. He stepped back slightly, putting a careful distance between them, though he didn't release her hand. "Should we... walk? I want to know everything about you. Where you've been, what you've seen, how you've lived all this time."

Leora nodded, grateful for the reprieve even as part of her mourned the space he'd created. "Yes. I'll show you the gardens. All of them."

They set off together, hand in hand, leaving the tree and its forbidden fruit behind. As they walked, Leora couldn't help but notice how different everything looked with Theren beside her. The paths seemed narrower, more intimate. The falling leaves seemed to fall *for* them rather than simply falling.

Or perhaps it was just that she was seeing it all through new eyes. Eyes that had finally found something—someone—worth looking at besides endless, unchanging perfection.

***

Later that afternoon, Theren led Leora to a clearing in the winter garden where he'd been working on something.

"I wanted to show you this," he said, gesturing to a structure made of stones—not stacked in the Garden's usual perfect symmetry, but arranged in a spiral pattern that seemed to flow and move even though the stones were still.

"You made this?" Leora asked, circling it slowly. The pattern was beautiful but also slightly unsettling, like it suggested movement in a place where everything was supposed to stay frozen.

"I've been trying to for weeks," Theren admitted. "Every time I get it right, the Garden—" He stopped, jaw tightening. "Watch."

He placed another stone carefully at the spiral's edge, completing the pattern. For a moment, it held. The spiral was perfect, organic, full of life and intention.

Then the stone trembled.

Before Leora's eyes, it shifted slightly—just an inch—but enough to break the pattern's flow. And once one stone moved, others followed, each one sliding just enough to transform Theren's spiral back into the Garden's preferred symmetry: neat, ordered, dead.

Theren's hands clenched into fists. "Every time. I build something that feels right, that feels alive, the Garden undoes it. Forces it back into—into whatever safe, frozen version it prefers."

Leora stared at the ruined spiral, understanding flooding through her. "It's not just me," she said quietly. "You feel it too. The wrongness. The control."

"I thought I was alone in it," Theren said. "Thought maybe something was wrong with me for wanting—" He gestured helplessly at the stones. "For wanting to make something that wasn't perfect. That was mine."

Leora reached for his hand. "Nothing's wrong with you. The Garden is what's wrong. It won't let anything change. Won't let anything grow."

"The tree let me touch it," Theren said, his voice dropping. "The eternal tree. I tried once, before I met you, and it didn't stop me. That's the only thing in this entire Garden that feels like it has its own will. Like it's not controlled."

"Maybe that's what drew us both there," Leora suggested. "The only thing in the Garden that's really alive. Really free."

They stood together looking at the ruined spiral, and Leora felt something settle between them—a shared recognition. They were both prisoners here. Both hungry for something the Garden would never provide.

"Build it again," she said suddenly. "The spiral. Let me help you."

"The Garden will just—"

"I know. But build it anyway. Keep building it. Every time it breaks, build it again." Leora squeezed his hand. "That's choosing, isn't it? Refusing to accept what we're given. Insisting on making something of our own, even if it doesn't last."

Theren looked at her for a long moment, then smiled—small but genuine. "Alright. Let's build it together."

They knelt side by side and began rearranging the stones. The Garden would undo their work, Leora knew. But for now, for this moment, they were creating something that was theirs.

And that mattered.

"Tell me about the winter garden," she said as they crossed from fall into summer, the air warming noticeably around them. "I've only been there a few times. It felt... lonely."

"It is lonely," Theren said. "Everything is covered in snow that never melts. Ice that never thaws. It's beautiful, but it's also—" He paused, seeming to choose his words carefully. "Sterile. Nothing grows there. Nothing changes. It's just cold and quiet and still."

"Like time stopped," Leora murmured, understanding instinctively what he meant.

"Exactly." He glanced at her, surprise and recognition flickering across his face. "You understand."

"All the gardens are like that, in their own way. Frozen in their season. Never becoming anything else." She led him around a cluster of peach trees heavy with fruit, then through a meadow of wildflowers that grew in suspiciously perfect rows. "I used to think it was peaceful. Now it just feels..."

"Wrong," Theren finished for her.

"Yes."

They walked in comfortable silence for a while, their joined hands swinging slightly between them. Leora found herself acutely aware of every point of contact—the way their palms pressed together, the way their fingers interlaced, the calluses on his hand that felt different from her own. She'd never thought about hands before, never paid attention to them as anything other than tools for picking fruit or weaving grass.

Now she couldn't stop thinking about what else they might do. Where else they might touch.

The thought made heat rush through her body, settling low in her belly in a way that was entirely new and slightly alarming.

"Leora?" Theren's voice pulled her from her thoughts. "Are you alright? Your hand just got very warm."

She felt her face flush. "I'm fine. Just thinking."

"About what?" There was curiosity in his tone, but also something else. Something that suggested he might be having similar thoughts.

"About..." She hesitated, then decided honesty was easier than evasion. "About touching. About what it felt like when we first... when our hands—" She gestured helplessly with her free hand. "I don't understand what that was."

Theren stopped walking, pulling her to a stop beside him. They were at the border between summer and spring now, standing in that strange liminal space where the air couldn't decide whether to be warm or cool. He turned to face her, and the look in his eyes made her stomach flip.

"It wasn't just me, then," he said quietly. "When I touched you, I felt—" He shook his head, struggling with words. "Like lightning. Like fire. Like something woke up inside me that I didn't know was sleeping."

"Yes," Leora breathed. "Exactly like that."

They stared at each other, and Leora could see his pulse beating in his throat, fast and hard. Could see the way his chest rose and fell with each breath. Could see the way he was looking at her mouth again, longer this time, with clear intent.

"Can I—" He swallowed hard. "Can I try something?"

Her heart was racing now, her whole body humming with anticipation. "Yes."

Slowly, carefully, Theren raised his free hand and reached toward her face. Leora held perfectly still, watching his fingers approach, her breath caught somewhere between her lungs and her throat.

His fingertips brushed her cheek, feather-light, and that lightning sensation exploded through her again. But this time she was ready for it, this time she leaned into it, closing her eyes and letting the feeling wash over her.

His touch was gentle, exploratory, as if he was learning the geography of her face. He traced the line of her cheekbone, then her jaw, then—so softly she almost couldn't feel it—the curve of her lower lip.

Leora's eyes flew open, and she found him staring at her with an expression she couldn't quite read. Awe, maybe. Or hunger. Or both.

"Your skin is so soft," he whispered. "I've never felt anything like it."

She wanted to say something witty or wise, but all she could manage was, "You can touch me. More, I mean. If you want to."

Something darkened in his eyes. Not threatening, but deeper, more intense. "I want to," he said, his voice rough. "I want to touch all of you. I want to understand how you're made, what makes you smile, what makes you gasp like that—"

He must have noticed her sharp intake of breath at his words, because he stopped talking abruptly, his hand stilling against her face.

"Don't stop," Leora whispered, surprising herself with her own boldness.

Theren's hand slid from her cheek to the side of her neck, his palm warm against her racing pulse. His thumb brushed the hollow of her throat, and she couldn't suppress the small sound that escaped her.

"Like that," he murmured, something like wonder in his voice. "That sound. I want to learn what causes it."

Leora's whole body was trembling now, her knees weak, her mind spinning. Every place he touched felt like it was catching fire, and she wanted more, wanted his hands everywhere, wanted to press herself against him and see if that would somehow satisfy this aching hunger that was building inside her.

But before she could move, before she could close the distance between them, the sky darkened suddenly.

They both looked up, startled. Clouds had rolled in from nowhere—thick, black, roiling clouds that seemed to boil with anger. Thunder rumbled, loud and close, and the temperature dropped so quickly that Leora began shivering.

"The Keeper," Theren said, his hand falling away from her neck, but his other hand still gripping hers tightly. "It's warning us again."

As if in confirmation, the wind picked up, tearing through the trees with violence. Branches creaked and groaned. Flowers doubled over, their petals scattering. Even the fruit began to fall, thudding to the ground in a way that felt less like natural ripeness and more like abandonment.

This is not innocence, the Keeper's voice echoed through the Garden, through the storm, through their very bones. *This is awareness. This is the beginning of knowledge. Turn back now, while you still can.*

Leora pressed closer to Theren instinctively, and his arm came around her shoulders, pulling her against his side. The contact, so much more than just their hands, sent sensation flooding through her despite the fear, despite the storm.

"We haven't done anything wrong," Leora called out to the empty air, her voice shaking but defiant. "We're just—we're just learning each other."

Learning leads to wanting. Wanting leads to taking. Taking leads to the fall.

The words hit like physical blows, each one heavy with inevitability.

"What if we don't care?" Theren shouted, and Leora could feel the anger vibrating through his chest where she pressed against him. "What if we choose this? Choose each other? Choose wanting?"

The Garden went deathly still. The wind stopped. The thunder ceased. Even the leaves suspended their falling, hanging in mid-air like the world itself was holding its breath.

When the Keeper's voice came again, it was quieter, sadder, resigned:

Then you choose to leave innocence behind. And innocence, once lost, can never be reclaimed.

The leaves began to fall again, slowly now, like tears. The clouds remained, but the violence went out of them. And beneath it all, Leora could feel something fundamental shifting in the Garden itself—as if it was rearranging itself around their choice, accepting the inevitability of what they'd set in motion.

Theren looked down at her, still holding her against his side, and something passed between them. An understanding. A commitment.

"I don't want innocence," Leora said, speaking not to the Keeper but to him. "Not if innocence means staying asleep. Not if it means living without knowing you."

"Neither do I," Theren replied, his arm tightening around her shoulders.

They stood there in the strange, sad rain of falling leaves, holding each other as the Garden mourned something they didn't entirely understand yet. But beneath the fear and the confusion, Leora felt something else growing. Something bright and fierce and undeniable.

She felt alive.

And that, she was beginning to understand, was worth any price.

"Come on," Theren said finally, his voice gentle. "Let's find shelter. We should talk. Actually talk. About what's happening, what we want, what comes next."

Leora nodded, reluctant to step away from the warmth of his body but knowing he was right. They needed to think, to plan, to understand what they were choosing before they went any further.

But as they walked hand in hand toward the spring garden, where Leora knew of a grove with thick-canopied trees that might shield them from the weather, she couldn't shake the feeling that it might already be too late for thinking and planning.

The wanting had already begun.

And once you started wanting, once you tasted that first drop of desire, how could you ever stop?

Chapter Four

What Lives Between Words

The grove Leora led them to was in the heart of the spring garden, where ancient willows bent over a clear stream like protective guardians. Their branches hung low and thick, creating a natural shelter that filtered the gray light into something softer, greener, almost underwater.

Theren ducked beneath the lowest branches and looked around, his expression shifting from wariness to wonder. "I've never been here before."

"It's one of my favorite places," Leora said, settling onto a patch of moss near the stream. The water babbled over smooth stones, a gentle sound that had always soothed her restlessness. "When I needed to think, I'd come here. Before I found the tree."

Theren sat beside her—not quite touching, but close enough that she could feel the heat radiating from his body. The space between them felt charged, heavy with possibility and restraint in equal measure.

For a long moment, neither of them spoke. The sound of the stream filled the silence, along with the occasional drip of condensation from the willow leaves above. The storm had passed, but left the air thick with moisture, everything damp and glistening.

"I'm afraid," Leora said finally, the words tumbling out before she could stop them. "Of what's happening. Of what we're choosing. Of how much I want something I don't even understand."

Theren turned to look at her, his blue eyes serious. "I'm afraid too. But I'm more afraid of going back to being alone. Of pretending you don't exist." He paused, his jaw working as if he was trying to find the right words. "All my life, I thought contentment was enough. I didn't know there was anything else to feel. But now—"

"Now you're awake," Leora finished softly.

"Yes." He reached out slowly and took her hand again, that now-familiar lightning sparking between their palms. "And I don't want to go back to sleep. Even if being awake hurts."

Leora threaded her fingers through his, studying their joined hands. His were larger, his fingers longer, the skin rougher as if he'd spent more time working with stone or wood than she had. "Tell me about your life. Before me. What did you do? How did you spend your days?"

A small smile tugged at his lips. "I built things, mostly. The Keeper would show me visions of what it wanted—a stone circle here, a pathway there, a shelter for the deer in the winter garden. And I'd build them." He gestured with his free hand as he spoke, and Leora found herself watching the movement, fascinated by the strength in his forearms, the way his muscles shifted beneath his skin. "I thought I was creating. Now I realize I was just... following instructions."

"I wove," Leora offered. "Baskets, mats, coverings. I'd gather materials from all the gardens and weave them into patterns that seemed to come to me in dreams. But you're right—they weren't my patterns. They were the Keeper's." She felt a surge of anger at the realization. "Everything we did, everything we made, it was all guided. Controlled."

"We were puppets," Theren said, his voice hardening. "Beautiful, content puppets in a perfect prison."

The words settled between them, ugly and true.

Leora shifted closer to him, needing the contact, needing to feel something real and unchosen. "What do you remember from before? From your earliest memories?"

Theren was quiet for a long moment, his thumb absently stroking the back of her hand. "Waking up in the winter garden. Snow falling. The Keeper's voice telling me I was home, I was safe, I was exactly where I belonged." He met her eyes. "But I don't remember being born. Don't remember being a child. It's like I just... appeared, fully formed."

"Same," Leora whispered, a chill running through her despite the humid air. "I woke up in the summer garden. The Keeper told me I'd always been there, would always be there. And I just... accepted it. Never questioned where I came from or why."

"Until recently."

"Until the chill started." She pressed her free hand to her chest, over her heart. "This feeling that something was wrong. That I was missing something."

Theren's gaze followed her hand, lingering on the rise and fall of her chest, then flicking back to her face with visible effort. "I felt it too. A restlessness. A hunger that had nothing to do with food." His voice dropped lower. "I started having dreams."

Leora's breath caught. "What kind of dreams?"

He hesitated, color rising in his cheeks. "Of being touched. Of touching. Of skin against skin in ways that felt—" He shook his head. "I'd wake up and my body would feel strange. Hot. Aching. I didn't understand it."

Heat flooded through Leora's body at his words. "I dreamed too," she admitted, her voice barely above a whisper. "Of hands in my hair. Of breath on my neck. Of wanting something I couldn't name."

The air between them thickened again, that familiar charge building. Theren's gaze dropped to her mouth, then to her throat where her pulse was visibly racing.

"Is it like this for you?" he asked roughly. "Right now? This feeling like your skin is too tight and your blood is too hot, and all you can think about is—"

"Touching," Leora breathed. "Yes. All I can think about is touching you."

They stared at each other, the confession hanging in the air between them like a living thing.

"We should be careful," Theren said, though his body was already shifting closer to hers. "The Keeper warned us. Learning leads to wanting. Wanting leads to—"

"I'm already wanting," Leora interrupted, surprising herself with her boldness. "From the moment I saw you. Maybe even before. Maybe that's what the dreams were. My body knowing you were out there somewhere, waiting for me to find you."

Theren made a sound low in his throat, half groan, half laugh. "You're making it very difficult to be cautious."

"Maybe I don't want to be cautious." She released his hand and turned to face him fully, kneeling on the moss so they were at eye level. "Maybe I want to understand this. To learn what happens when we touch without fear."

"Leora—"

"Please." She reached up slowly, giving him time to pull away, and placed her palm against his chest. Even through the contact, she could feel his heart racing, matching the frantic rhythm of her own. "Teach me. Or let me teach you. Or let us learn together."

For a moment, Theren sat frozen, his eyes locked on hers, something like agony and ecstasy warring in his expression. Then his restraint broke.

He raised both hands to her face, cradling it gently, his thumbs brushing over her cheekbones. The lightning sensation was immediate and overwhelming, but this time she didn't gasp or pull away. She leaned into it, her eyes fluttering closed, her whole world narrowing to the points where his skin met hers.

"You're so beautiful," he murmured, his voice rough with wonder. "I don't think the Garden ever made anything as beautiful as you."

Leora's eyes opened, and she found him watching her with such intensity it made her chest ache. Slowly, carefully, she raised her own hands to mirror his position, cupping his face, feeling the slight scratch of stubble against her palms, the warmth of his skin, the sharp line of his jaw.

"You too," she whispered. "You're—I don't have words for what you are."

They stayed like that for a long moment, simply holding each other's faces, learning the geography of cheekbones and jawlines and the tender skin beneath eyes. It was intimate in a way that made Leora's throat tight, made her feel seen and known in a way she'd never experienced.

Then Theren's thumb brushed over her lower lip, and her mouth parted instinctively.

The small movement seemed to undo something in him. His gaze darkened, dropped to her mouth, and stayed there. "Can I—" His voice cracked slightly. "I want to kiss you. Is that—would that be—"

"Yes," Leora breathed, already tilting her face toward his. "Yes."

Theren closed the distance between them slowly, giving her every chance to change her mind. But Leora didn't want to change her mind. She wanted this more than she'd ever wanted anything.

When their lips met, it was nothing like the gentle touches they'd shared so far. This was lightning and fire and something that felt like the world remaking itself. Theren's mouth was warm and soft and searching, moving against hers in a way that made her whole body arch toward him.

Leora had no idea what she was doing, but her body seemed to know instinctively. Her lips parted further, and when

Theren's tongue touched hers tentatively, experimentally, the sensation that shot through her was so intense she made a sound she'd never made before—something between a gasp and a moan.

Theren pulled back slightly, his breathing ragged. "Was that—did I hurt you?"

"No." Leora grabbed the front of his chest, pulling him back. "Don't stop. Please don't stop."

He kissed her again, deeper this time, less tentative. His hands slid from her face to tangle in her hair, tilting her head to give him better access, and Leora's hands roamed over his shoulders, his back, learning the shape of him through touch.

The kiss went on and on, building in intensity, until they were both trembling with it. Leora found herself pressing closer, wanting to feel more of him, wanting to eliminate any space between their bodies. Theren seemed to have the same idea because his hands dropped to her waist, pulling her against him until she was practically in his lap.

The full-body contact was almost too much. Everywhere they touched felt like it was burning, like every nerve ending was firing at once. Leora could feel the rapid rise and fall of Theren's chest, the heat of his body, the way his hands gripped her waist like he was afraid she might disappear.

When they finally broke apart, both gasping for air, Leora realized she was shaking. Her entire body felt like it had been struck by lightning, every part of her alive and aware and wanting more.

Theren rested his forehead against hers, his breath coming in harsh pants. "I think—" He paused, swallowing hard. "I think I understand now. What the Keeper meant. About wanting."

"It doesn't stop, does it?" Leora whispered. "Now that we've started."

"No." His hands were still on her waist, his thumbs tracing small circles on her bare skin. "I don't think it does."

They stayed like that, foreheads pressed together, breathing each other's air, trying to calm their racing hearts. But beneath the attempt at restraint, Leora could feel the want still pulsing between them, hungry and insistent.

"We should probably—" Theren started.

A sound from beyond the willow branches cut him off. Not loud, but distinct. A rustling that didn't match the wind, a sense of movement that felt deliberate.

They both froze, turning toward the noise.

Through the hanging branches, Leora caught a glimpse of something that made her breath stop entirely. A shape, sinuous and fluid, moving along the streambank. Silver-black scales that caught the filtered light. A head that rose, turned, and for one heart-stopping moment, seemed to look directly at her.

Eyes like polished obsidian met hers, and in them, Leora saw something that looked almost like recognition. Almost like approval.

Then the creature—the serpent, because that's what it was, unmistakably—slipped into the underbrush and disappeared.

"Did you see that?" Leora breathed.

Theren's arms had come around her protectively, pulling her back against his chest. "What was it?"

"I don't know." But even as she said it, Leora felt a strange pull toward where the serpent had vanished. Not fear, exactly. Curiosity. Recognition of something that shouldn't be familiar but somehow was.

"We should go," Theren said, tension in his voice. "If there are dangerous creatures in the Garden now—"

"I don't think it's dangerous." Leora turned in his arms to face him. "At least, not to us. Did you see its eyes? It looked at me like..." She trailed off, unable to articulate the feeling.

"Like what?"

"Like it knew me. Like it was waiting for me."

Theren's expression tightened with worry. "That's exactly what concerns me."

But Leora couldn't shake the feeling that the serpent's appearance wasn't a threat. It was an invitation.

To what, she didn't yet know.

But as they left the grove hand in hand, as the spring garden gave way to summer and the light shifted from green-filtered to gold, Leora felt certain of one thing:

The serpent would appear again. And when it did, she would be ready to hear whatever it had to say.

Chapter Five

The Serpent's Gift

Leora couldn't stop thinking about the serpent.

Three days had passed since they'd seen it by the stream—three days of exploring the gardens together, of stolen kisses under fruit trees, of learning the taste and texture of each other's skin. Three days of the Garden growing stranger around them, more wild, less predictable. Flowers bloomed out of season. Fruit ripened and fell without warning. The paths rearranged themselves overnight, forcing Leora and Theren to navigate by instinct rather than memory.

The Keeper's presence had withdrawn to a distant hum, like disappointment held at arm's length. It watched but did not speak. It maintained but did not guide. The silence felt like punishment and freedom in equal measure.

But through it all, Leora kept returning in her mind to those obsidian eyes, to the sense of recognition that had passed between her and the serpent. She found herself scanning the underbrush as they walked, looking for that flash of silver-black scales, that sinuous movement.

Theren had noticed her distraction.

"You're thinking about it again," he said as they sat together in the autumn garden, sharing a lunch of figs and late-season berries. His hand rested on her knee, a casual intimacy they'd fallen into naturally. "The creature."

Leora didn't deny it. "Don't you wonder what it was? Where it came from? Why we'd never seen anything like it before?"

"I wonder if it's connected to all of this." Theren gestured at the garden around them, at the leaves that fell in patterns that seemed almost deliberate, at the way the light had taken on a golden, melancholy quality. "To the changes. To us."

"What if it is?" Leora plucked a berry from her palm and ate it, the tartness making her wince slightly. "What if it's part of what's supposed to happen?"

Theren's hand tightened on her knee. "The Keeper warned us about knowledge. About choosing awareness over innocence. What if that creature is—" He paused, searching for words. "What if it's dangerous? What if it wants to lead us somewhere we shouldn't go?"

Leora turned to look at him fully, studying the concern in his blue eyes, the protective set of his shoulders. "And what if it wants to show us something true? Something the Keeper has been hiding from us?"

A flicker of unease crossed Theren's face. "You sound like you want to find it."

"Maybe I do." The admission surprised her, but once spoken, it felt right. "The Keeper has controlled everything about our lives. Our work, our paths, our very existence. What if there's something else out there? Someone else who can tell us the truth?"

"Or someone who will lie to us," Theren countered, his voice tight. "The Keeper has protected us. Fed us. Kept us safe. Why would we trust a creature we just met over the force that's cared for us our entire lives?"

It was the first real disagreement they'd had, and the tension of it sat heavy between them. Leora felt a flash of frustration—at him for being so accepting, at herself for wanting to push boundaries, at the whole situation that had turned something as simple as curiosity into a source of conflict.

"I'm not saying we should trust it," she said carefully. "I'm saying we should at least try to understand it. To understand everything that's happening."

Theren was quiet for a long moment, his thumb tracing absent circles on her knee. When he spoke again, his voice was softer. "I'm afraid. Of losing you. Of losing this." He gestured between them. "Of making choices that lead somewhere we can't come back from."

Leora's frustration melted into tenderness. She reached up and cupped his face, feeling the familiar spark of contact, the warmth that never quite faded. "I'm afraid too. But I'm more afraid of staying ignorant. Of letting fear keep us from understanding our own lives."

He leaned into her touch, his eyes closing briefly. "Promise me something?"

"What?"

"That we'll be careful. That we won't rush toward danger just because it's new or exciting or—" He opened his eyes and looked at her intently. "—or because it promises answers to questions we might not want answered."

Leora wanted to promise. Wanted to give him that reassurance. But something in her rebelled against making a vow she wasn't sure she could keep.

"I promise I won't do anything reckless," she said finally. "And I promise we'll face whatever comes together."

It wasn't quite what he'd asked for, and they both knew it. But Theren nodded, accepting it, and pulled her close for a kiss that tasted like worry and want in equal measure.

***

That night, Leora couldn't sleep.

She lay beside Theren on the bed of moss and woven grass they'd made together in the Garden of the Fall, listening to his deep, even breathing, watching the way moonlight filtered through the tree's eternal leaves to paint patterns on his skin.

They hadn't made love yet—hadn't even come close, though the wanting was there every time they touched. Some unspoken agreement held them back, a sense that crossing that final boundary would change something irrevocable. That once they gave themselves to each other completely, there would be no returning to anything resembling innocence.

But lying here beside him, feeling the warmth of his body, hearing the sound of his breath, Leora felt that boundary growing thinner with each passing day.

She carefully extracted herself from his loose embrace and stood, shivering slightly in the night chill. The tree loomed above her, its dark fruit gleaming in the moonlight like promises or warnings. She'd grown so accustomed to its presence that she barely registered the sweet, intoxicating scent anymore.

Almost.

Tonight it seemed stronger, more insistent, making her head feel light and her body feel heavy.

Leora walked away from their sleeping spot, following no particular path, just moving because staying still felt impossible. The Garden of the Fall was different at night—quieter, but somehow more alive. Shadows moved in ways that suggested more than wind. The falling leaves caught moonlight as they spiraled down, each one a tiny silver dancer.

She found herself drawn to the base of the tree, to the massive roots that spread like reaching fingers across the earth. She'd spent so much time here lately that she knew every ridge and hollow, every place where the bark had smoothed with age or roughened with weather.

Which is why she noticed immediately when something was different.

There, tucked between two roots in a spot she was certain had been empty yesterday, lay something that gleamed with an otherworldly sheen. Leora crouched down, her heart beginning to race, and reached for it with trembling fingers.

The moment she touched it, she knew what it was.

Skin. Serpent skin. Shed and left behind like a gift or a message.

It was impossibly smooth, cool to the touch, with scales that caught the moonlight and scattered it in rainbow patterns. The entire length was intact—easily as long as she was tall—and when she lifted it, it weighed almost nothing, as if it were made of solidified moonlight rather than anything substantial.

Leora sat back on her heels, cradling the shed skin in her hands, and felt something shift in her chest. Not the chill she'd lived with for so long, but something warmer. Something that felt like recognition, like coming home to a place she'd never been.

The skin pulsed faintly in her hands—not with life exactly, but with something. Memory, maybe. Or potential. Or the echo of whatever creature had worn it.

She should show Theren. Should wake him up and tell him what she'd found, let him see it, let them decide together what it meant.

But even as the thought formed, Leora knew she wouldn't.

This felt private. Personal. Like it had been left specifically for her, and sharing it would somehow diminish whatever message or meaning it carried.

She stood slowly, the snakeskin carefully, and looked around for somewhere to hide it. Her eyes landed on the woven satchel she used for gathering—the one she'd made herself, with no guidance from the Keeper, during those early days when the chill first started.

Carefully, reverently, Leora folded the serpent skin until it was small enough to fit inside the satchel, then tucked it beneath a layer of gathered moss and dried leaves. Her hands were shaking as she tied the satchel closed, her heart racing with something that felt like guilt and exhilaration mixed together.

She'd kept her first secret from Theren.

The weight of it settled in her stomach like a stone, but beneath the guilt was something else. A sense of her own separateness. Her own agency. She loved Theren—was beginning to understand that's what this feeling was—but she was also her own person. She could have things that were just hers. Thoughts, feelings, secrets.

The realization felt both terrifying and liberating.

When she returned to their sleeping spot, Theren had shifted in his sleep, one arm reaching across the space where she'd been as if searching for her. Leora carefully lay back down beside him, and his arm immediately came around her, pulling her close even in sleep.

She fit against him perfectly, her back to his chest, his breath warm on her neck. Safe. Cherished. But also, now, separate in a way she hadn't been before.

The serpent's skin pulsed gently in her satchel several feet away, and Leora closed her eyes, trying to quiet her racing thoughts.

Tomorrow, she would be normal. Tomorrow, she would push away the guilt and the curiosity and focus on Theren, on what they were building together.

But tonight, lying in the darkness with a secret pressed against her heart, Leora felt something she'd never felt before.

She felt powerful.

***

The next morning brought rain—real rain, not the gentle mist that sometimes drifted through the gardens but actual rain that drummed against leaves and turned the earth to mud. Leora had never seen it before. The Garden had always been perfectly climate-controlled, never too wet or too dry.

She and Theren huddled beneath the tree's canopy, which somehow stayed mostly dry despite the deluge around them. The fruit above them seemed to glow more brightly in the gray light, and that sweet scent intensified until Leora had to breathe through her mouth to keep from feeling dizzy.

"This is new," Theren said, watching water stream past their shelter. "I've never seen the Garden angry like this."

"Maybe it's not anger," Leora suggested. "Maybe it's grief."

Theren looked at her sharply. "Grief for what?"

"For losing us. For watching us change into something it can't control anymore."

He was quiet for a moment, then reached for her hand. "Do you regret it? Any of it?"

"No." The answer came without hesitation. "Do you?"

"No." He pulled her closer, tucking her against his side. "Though I wish I understood what happens next. Where this is leading us."

Leora thought of the serpent skin hidden in her satchel, of the secret burning in her chest. "Maybe we're not meant to understand yet. Maybe we just have to keep choosing."

"Choosing what?"

"Each other. Awareness. Truth." She paused, then added softly, "Freedom."

The rain intensified, and somewhere in the distance, thunder rolled. But here, beneath the tree that refused to bend or shed or acknowledge the storm, they were dry and warm and together.

Theren tilted Leora's face up and kissed her, slow and deep, and she felt the now-familiar lightning spark between them. His hands roamed her back, her sides, learning the shape of her body. She arched into the touch, wanting more, always wanting more.

When they finally broke apart, both breathing hard, Theren rested his forehead against hers. "I love you," he said quietly. "I don't know if that's the right word for this feeling, but it's the closest I can find."

Leora's heart swelled painfully in her chest. "I love you too."

It was the first time either of them had said it aloud, and the words hung in the air between them, bright and fragile and true.

The rain continued to fall, and the Garden continued to change, and in her satchel, the serpent's skin pulsed with secrets waiting to be discovered.

But for this moment, Leora let herself simply be held, simply be loved, simply be with someone who saw her and chose her despite all the uncertainty.

The secrets could wait.

The serpent could wait.

Everything could wait except this—the warmth of his body, the taste of his mouth, the sound of his voice saying he loved her.

Everything else could wait.

But deep down, Leora knew it wouldn't wait forever.

Chapter Six

The Storm's Answer

The rain stopped as abruptly as it had begun, leaving the Garden steaming in sudden sunlight. Everything dripped and glistened, the air thick with the scent of wet earth and bruised fruit. Leora and Theren emerged from beneath the tree's shelter to find the world transformed.

Mushrooms had sprouted overnight—not the neat, edible varieties Leora was used to, but strange twisted things in colors that seemed wrong. Brilliant purple with spots of luminescent green. Deep crimson bleeding to black. One cluster near the base of a fallen log looked almost like tiny hands reaching toward the sky.

"I don't think we should eat those," Theren said, eyeing them warily.

Leora crouched down to examine them more closely, fascinated despite herself. The serpent's skin in her satchel—which she'd been careful to keep close—seemed to pulse in response to the mushrooms' presence, as if recognizing something kindred in their strangeness.

"The Garden is changing faster now," she said. "Every day something new. Something wild."

"Or something wrong." Theren reached down and pulled her to her feet, his hand lingering on her arm. "We should be careful about what we touch. What we eat. What we trust."

There it was again—that note of caution, of wanting to maintain control in a situation that was rapidly spinning beyond their grasp. Leora understood his fear, even shared it on some level, but part of her thrilled at the chaos. At the sense that the Garden's perfect order was finally cracking, revealing something raw and real beneath.

They walked hand in hand toward the spring garden, where Theren had left some of his building tools near a half-finished stone circle the Keeper had once commissioned. But when they arrived at the clearing, they both stopped short.

The stones had been rearranged.

Not scattered or destroyed, but deliberately moved into a different pattern. Instead of the neat circle the Keeper had envisioned, they now formed something more organic—a spiral that curved in on itself, drawing the eye toward a center point where the largest stone stood like a marker.

"I didn't do this," Theren said, his voice tight. "This isn't what the Keeper asked for."

Leora felt a chill run through her—not the old chill of restlessness, but something sharper. More immediate. "Maybe the Keeper didn't ask for it. Maybe the Garden is making its own choices now."

Before Theren could respond, the air shifted. The temperature dropped so suddenly that their breath misted in front of them. The birds fell silent. Even the insects stopped their humming.

And then the Keeper was there.

Not fully visible—it had never been fully visible—but more present than Leora had ever experienced. A shimmer in the air that suggested a form without quite achieving one. A pressure that felt like being watched by something vast and ancient and deeply concerned.

When it spoke, the voice resonated through their bones, through the earth itself:

You have strayed far from the path I laid for you.

Leora and Theren moved closer together instinctively, Theren's arm coming around her shoulders. She could feel his heart racing against her side, matching the frantic rhythm of her own.

"We've only sought to understand," Leora said, proud that her voice came out steady. "To know ourselves. Each other. Is that really straying?"

Understanding comes with time. With readiness. You rush toward knowledge you are not prepared to bear.

"How do you know we're not ready?" Theren asked, some of his earlier protectiveness giving way to defiance. "You've kept us separate our entire lives. Kept us ignorant of each other's existence. How do you know what we can handle?"

The air grew colder still, and the shimmer intensified. Leora could almost see a face in it now—features that suggested wisdom and sorrow and something that might have been fear.

I know because I have seen this story before. I have watched innocence give way to awareness, awareness to desire, desire to choice, and choice to suffering. I know where this path leads, and I sought to spare you both.

"Spare us from what?" Leora demanded. "From being alive? From feeling? From choosing our own way?"

From pain, the Keeper said, and for the first time, its voice carried a note of something almost like pleading. *From loss. From death itself. The knowledge you seek comes at a price you cannot imagine. Once paid, it can never be refunded.*

Leora felt Theren's arm tighten around her, felt his uncertainty warring with his love for her. She knew he was tempted by the Keeper's words, by the promise of safety and continued innocence. Part of her was tempted, too.

But the serpent's skin pulsed against her hip, hidden in her satchel, and Leora remembered that feeling of power, of having something that was hers alone. She remembered waking up, truly waking up, and realizing she'd been asleep her entire life.

"We're not asking to be spared," she said quietly. "We're asking to be free."

Freedom and safety cannot coexist. Choose one, and you sacrifice the other.

"Then we choose freedom," Theren said, and Leora's heart soared to hear him say it, to hear him choose her and their uncertain future over the Keeper's promise of protected eternity.

The shimmer contracted, pulling in on itself until it was almost a solid shape. Leora could see eyes now—ancient, sad, resigned.

Then I cannot protect you from what comes next. The Garden itself will test you. Your own desires will test you. And when you stand before the final choice, you will have only yourselves to rely upon.

"We'll rely on each other," Leora said, reaching for Theren's hand.

Will you? The question hung in the air like smoke. *Even when secrets divide you? Even when fear makes you strangers? Even when the wanting becomes so great it threatens to consume everything else?*

Leora felt her stomach drop. Did the Keeper know about the serpent's skin? About her deception?

But before she could respond, the Keeper's presence began to withdraw, the shimmer fading, the temperature slowly rising back toward normal.

I loved you both, the voice said, growing distant. *I still love you. But love that controls is not love at all. So I release you to your choices. And I will grieve what those choices cost.*

Then it was gone, leaving only the sound of water dripping from leaves and the gradual return of birdsong.

Leora and Theren stood in silence, both shaken, both trying to process what had just happened. The Keeper had given them permission—or absolution, or perhaps just an acknowledgment of its own powerlessness in the face of their determination.

They were truly free now.

And somehow that felt more terrifying than being controlled.

"Are you alright?" Theren asked finally, turning her to face him.

Leora nodded, though her hands were shaking. "I think so. Are you?"

Instead of answering, he pulled her close and kissed her. It was different from their other kisses—more desperate, more hungry, as if he needed to prove to himself that she was real and solid and still choosing him.

Leora kissed him back just as fiercely, her hands fisting in his hair, her body pressing against his. The Keeper's words echoed in her mind—*the wanting becomes so great it threatens to consume everything*—and she understood now what it had meant.

Because the wanting was consuming her. It lived in her skin, in her blood, in every breath and heartbeat. It made her reckless and bold and willing to risk anything for more of this feeling, more of him.

Theren's hands roamed her back, her sides, then lower, cupping her hips and pulling her impossibly closer. Leora gasped into his mouth, her whole body arching into the contact, and she felt something hard press against her stomach—his body responding to hers in a way she didn't fully understand but instinctively craved.

"Leora," he breathed against her lips, his voice rough with need. "We should—I don't know if we should—"

"Don't think," she whispered back, surprising herself with her boldness. "Please. I'm tired of thinking. Of being careful. I just want to feel."

His groan was answer enough. He kissed her deeper, his tongue exploring her mouth while his hands explored her body, learning every curve of her body. Leora's own hands wandered, tracing the muscles of his back, the breadth of his shoulders, the fascinating planes of his chest.

It wasn't enough. Nothing was enough. She wanted his skin against hers, wanted to understand how they fit together, wanted to chase this feeling to wherever it led.

As if reading her thoughts, Theren's hands moved lower, trembling, and Leora reached for him too, both of them—

Thunder cracked directly overhead, so loud and sudden that they both jumped apart.

The sky, which had been clear moments ago, was now filled with black clouds. Wind whipped through the clearing, bending trees that shouldn't bend, scattering stones from Theren's rearranged circle. The temperature plummeted again, but this time it felt different from the Keeper's presence.

This felt like the Garden itself was responding. Like the land and air and growing things were all rising up in protest.

Leora looked down and gasped. The ground beneath their feet was cracking, fissures spreading outward from where they stood. Grass withered and died in waves. Flowers that had been blooming moments ago collapsed in on themselves, petals browning and falling.

"What's happening?" Theren pulled her back from the spreading cracks, his face pale with shock.

"The Garden," Leora breathed. "It's reacting to us. To what we were about to—"

Another crack of thunder, and this time lightning struck close enough that they could feel the heat of it, could smell the ozone tang in the air. A tree at the edge of the clearing split down the middle, the two halves falling away from each other with a groan that sounded almost like pain.

Animals burst from the underbrush—deer, rabbits, birds taking flight in panicked clouds. All fleeing from the clearing, from them, as if they'd become the most dangerous things in the Garden.

The wind intensified, and Leora heard a voice in it—not the Keeper's voice, but something older, deeper, more primal. The voice of the Garden itself, maybe, or of the earth that held it:

Not yet. Not here. Not like this.

"We have to go," Theren said urgently, grabbing her hand and pulling her toward the path. "Now."

They ran, stumbling over newly formed roots that thrust up through the earth, dodging branches that seemed to reach for them. Behind them, the clearing continued to transform—more cracks spreading, more plants dying, the spiral of stones beginning to glow with a faint, ominous light.

They didn't stop running until they reached the Garden of the Fall, where the eternal tree stood unchanged, unmoved by the chaos around it. Only here did the wind calm, the thunder quiet, the sense of immediate danger recede.

Leora collapsed against one of the tree's massive roots, her heart hammering, her breath coming in gasps. Theren fell beside her, equally shaken, and for a long moment they just sat there trying to make sense of what had happened.

"The Garden tried to stop us," Leora said finally, her voice barely above a whisper. "When we were about to—when we almost—"

"I know." Theren's hand found hers, gripping tight. "It was like it knew. Like it could feel what we intended and refused to allow it."

Leora looked up at the tree above them, at the dark fruit hanging heavy on its branches. "Except here. The Garden didn't react here."

Theren followed her gaze, and understanding dawned in his eyes. "Because this place is already forbidden. Already outside the Keeper's control." He paused, then added quietly, "Or maybe this is exactly where it wants us. Where it's been drawing us all along."

They sat in silence, both processing the implications of that. The tree's sweet scent wrapped around them, stronger than ever in the aftermath of the storm. Leora's body still thrummed with frustrated desire, with the need Theren had awakened that had been so violently interrupted.

And from the corner of her eye, she saw something move in the shadows beneath the tree's far roots. A sinuous shape. Silver-black scales catching the light.

The serpent had returned.

It wound its way toward them slowly, deliberately, its obsidian eyes fixed on Leora. When it was perhaps ten feet away, it stopped and raised its head, regarding them both with what looked almost like curiosity.

Or expectation.

Theren tensed beside her, his protective instincts flaring, but Leora put a restraining hand on his arm. "Wait. I don't think it means us harm."

"How can you know that?"

Leora thought of the shed skin in her satchel, of the secret she'd been keeping, and felt guilt wash through her again. But stronger than guilt was curiosity. Need. The sense that this creature had answers they desperately required.

"I just do," she said softly.

The serpent's tongue flicked out, tasting the air. Then it spoke—not in words exactly, but in a way that resonated in their minds, clear and undeniable:

You seek to understand. I can teach you. But knowledge comes at a price. Are you willing to pay it?

Leora and Theren looked at each other, fear and desire and determination all swirling in the space between them.

"What price?" Theren asked warily.

The serpent's eyes seemed to gleam with something that might have been amusement.

Your innocence. Your safety. Your certainty that what you've been told is true.

"We've already lost those things," Leora said.

Have you? The serpent tilted its head. *Or have you only begun to lose them? There is much you still believe. Much you still trust. Much you still don't know to question.*

"Like what?" Leora demanded.

But the serpent was already retreating, sliding back into the shadows beneath the tree's roots.

Return tomorrow, its voice echoed in their minds. *Alone, Leora. And I will show you truths the Keeper never wanted you to see.*

Then it was gone, leaving them in the tree's shadow with more questions than answers and a desire still burning in their blood that had nowhere to go.

Theren turned to Leora, conflict clear in his eyes. "You're not actually considering it, are you? Going to see that creature alone?"

Leora touched the satchel at her hip, felt the serpent's skin pulse in response to her thoughts. She should tell him. Should confess that this wasn't the first contact, that she'd been hiding something from him.

But the words wouldn't come.

"I don't know," she said instead, which was both the truth and a lie together. "But I think... I think we need answers. And the Keeper clearly isn't going to give them to us."

Theren pulled her close, burying his face in her hair. "I'm afraid of losing you," he whispered. "To that creature. To knowledge I can't share. To a path I can't follow."

"You won't lose me," Leora promised, even as part of her wondered if that was a promise she could keep.

Because the wanting—for knowledge, for freedom, for the secrets the serpent promised—was growing just as strong as her wanting for Theren.

And she wasn't sure anymore which hunger would win.

Chapter Seven

Desire's Architecture

Leora waited until Theren's breathing deepened into sleep before she moved.

It was becoming easier to lie to him—not easier in her heart, which ached with every deception, but easier in practice. She'd learned to control her breathing, to keep her body relaxed even when her mind raced, to wait for that precise moment when he crossed from wakefulness into dreams.

She slipped from beneath his arm, moving with the careful stealth of prey avoiding a predator. Or perhaps she was the predator now. She wasn't sure anymore.

The night was warm, unusually so, as if the Garden itself was feverish. Leora gathered her satchel—the serpent's skin pulsing inside it like a second heartbeat—and made her way through the darkness toward the tree.

The moon was full, turning everything silver and strange. Shadows moved in ways that suggested intelligence, and more than once Leora thought she glimpsed eyes watching from the underbrush. But nothing approached her. Nothing hindered her path.

It was as if the Garden had been waiting for this.

When she reached the tree, the serpent was already there, coiled around one of the massive roots. Its scales caught the moonlight and scattered it in prismatic patterns, beautiful and hypnotic. Those obsidian eyes fixed on her as she approached, and Leora felt the weight of that gaze like a physical thing.

You came alone, the serpent's voice resonated in her mind, pleased. *Good. Some lessons require privacy.*

"Theren doesn't know I'm here," Leora admitted, guilt making her voice small.

I know. The serpent unwound itself slowly, sinuously, moving toward her with fluid grace. *You carry my gift with you. I can feel it.*

Leora's hand went instinctively to her satchel. "The skin. You left it for me."

I shed what no longer serves me. I thought you might benefit from understanding that concept. The serpent circled her slowly, not threatening but assessing. *You cling to things—safety, innocence, the Keeper's approval, even Theren's trust—when perhaps you should learn to shed them instead.*

"I love Theren," Leora said defensively. "I'm not clinging to him. I choose him."

Do you? The serpent completed its circle and raised its head to look directly into her eyes. *Or do you choose what he represents? Safety. Companionship. An excuse not to face the unknown alone?*

The words stung because they carried a grain of truth Leora didn't want to examine. "Why did you ask me here? What do you want to teach me?"

Everything. The serpent's tongue flicked out, tasting her fear, her curiosity, her hunger. *But we'll start with something simple. Something you already want to understand.*

"What?"

Desire. The word resonated through Leora's body, making her skin flush, her pulse quicken. *You feel it constantly now, don't you? For Theren. For knowledge. For more than this Garden can give you. But you don't understand what it is or where it leads.*

Leora thought of Theren's hands on her body, of the lightning that sparked wherever they touched, of the aching need that never seemed satisfied, no matter how much they kissed and explored each other. "Teach me, then."

The serpent led her deeper into the Garden of the Fall, to a place Leora had never seen before. A small clearing where the moonlight fell in a perfect circle, illuminating what looked like a natural pool of water so still it could have been glass.

Sit, the serpent commanded, and Leora obeyed, settling on the soft grass at the pool's edge.

The serpent coiled beside her, close enough that she could feel the coolness emanating from its scales. *Look into the water. Tell me what you see.*

Leora leaned forward and gazed into the pool. At first she saw only her own reflection—dark hair loose around her shoulders, eyes wide with apprehension and excitement. But as she continued to watch, the reflection began to change.

She saw herself as she'd been days ago, lying beside Theren, his hands exploring her body. She watched as memory-Leora arched into his touch, as her mouth opened in a silent gasp, as her own hands reached for him with desperate need.

"I see us," she whispered, heat flooding her face and body. "I see what we do together."

You see the surface, the serpent corrected. *Look deeper.*

Leora focused, and the image shifted. Now she could see inside the memory-bodies, could see something flowing between them like liquid light. It moved from Theren's hands into her skin, and from her skin back into him, a circuit of energy that grew brighter with each touch, each kiss, each moment of contact.

"What is that?" Leora breathed.

Life force. Essence. The energy that makes you more than just flesh and bone. The serpent's voice was like silk in her mind. *When you touch each other, you exchange it. Share it. Build it between you until it becomes something greater than either of you alone.*

The image shifted again, and now Leora saw what would happen if that circuit completed fully—if she and Theren gave themselves to each other without restraint. The light would build and build until it exploded outward, changing them both irrevocably. Making them something new.

That is what the Garden fears, the serpent continued. *Not your bodies joining, but what happens when they do. You would become creators yourselves. No longer the Keeper's children, but equals. Perhaps even rivals.*

"Is that why it stopped us?" Leora asked, remembering the violent reaction when they'd tried to go further. "Because we'd become too powerful?"

The Keeper prefers you dependent. Innocent. Controlled. The serpent circled the pool, its movements hypnotic. *But you were never meant to stay that way. You were meant to grow, to learn, to become. That is what it means to be truly alive.*

Leora tore her gaze from the pool to look at the serpent directly. "How do you know all this? What are you?"

The serpent's eyes gleamed with something that might have been amusement. *I am what happens when a creature chooses knowledge over contentment. I was once like you—kept, protected, controlled. But I learned to ask questions. To seek truths the Keeper preferred to hide. And for that, I was cast out of the perfect places and made to dwell in the wild ones.*

"Cast out," Leora repeated, a chill running through her. "Like a punishment?"

Like a liberation. The serpent moved closer, until its head was level with hers. *Tell me, Leora. Would you rather live forever in a beautiful cage, or die eventually having truly lived? Would you rather be safe and ignorant, or free and aware?*

The questions echoed the ones Leora had been asking herself since the chill first started, since she woke up and realized she'd been asleep. "Free and aware. But Theren—"

Theren wants safety. He says he chooses you, chooses freedom, but when the moment comes to truly commit, to truly risk everything, what will he choose then?

"He loves me," Leora insisted, but doubt crept into her voice.

Does love mean giving you what you want, or protecting you from what you might become? The serpent tilted its head. *He would keep you safe. Keep you his. But safety and possession often wear the same face.*

Leora wanted to argue, to defend Theren, but she remembered his hesitation, his fear, his constant worry about what they might lose. She loved him for his protectiveness, but she also chafed against it.

Look again, the serpent commanded, gesturing to the pool with its tail.

This time, the water showed Leora a different scene. Herself and Theren standing before the tree, the dark fruit hanging within reach. In this vision, Leora reached for it, but Theren caught her wrist, pulled her hand back, and held her away from the choice she wanted to make.

"No," Leora whispered. "He wouldn't—"

Wouldn't he? The serpent's voice was gentle now, almost pitying. *When choosing between you and safety, between your desire for knowledge and his desire to protect you, which do you think he'll choose?*

The vision shifted again. Now she saw herself alone, reaching for the fruit unhindered. The moment her fingers closed around it, that circuit of light she'd seen before exploded through her body, transforming her from within. When she turned to face the viewer, her eyes blazed with knowledge and power.

She looked beautiful. Terrifying. Free.

That is what you could become, the serpent said. *If you're brave enough to choose it. If you're willing to risk everything—even him—for the truth.*

Leora pulled back from the pool, her heart racing, her mind reeling. "You're trying to divide us. To make me doubt him."

I'm trying to show you what you already know but won't admit. The serpent coiled back into its original position. *You and Theren want different things. You want truth. He wants safety. You want to become. He wants you to stay. Eventually, you'll have to choose between his love and your freedom.*

"That's not fair," Leora said, her voice breaking. "Why can't I have both?"

Because truly loving someone means letting them become who they're meant to be, even if it terrifies you. Even if it changes them beyond recognition. Even if it means losing them. The serpent's gaze softened slightly. *Does Theren love you enough to let you go? Do you love him enough to leave if you must?*

Leora couldn't answer. The questions cut too deep, exposed truths she wasn't ready to face.

The serpent seemed to sense her turmoil. *You don't have to decide tonight. But soon, very soon, you'll stand before a choice that can't be unmade. And when that moment comes, you need to know what you truly want. Not what the Keeper wants for you. Not what Theren wants for you. What you want for yourself.*

"I want to understand," Leora whispered. "Everything. Even if it hurts. Even if it costs me."

Then keep coming to me. Keep learning. Keep questioning. The serpent began to uncoil, preparing to depart. *But know this: the more you learn, the wider the gulf between you and Theren will grow. Knowledge shared is knowledge diluted. Some truths can only be understood alone.*

"Wait," Leora called out as the serpent began to slide away. "What about the fruit? The tree? When do I—when should we—"

When you're ready, the serpent said simply. *You'll know. Your body will tell you. The hunger will become undeniable, and on that day, you'll have to choose: feed it, or starve forever.*

Then it was gone, disappeared into the shadows, leaving Leora alone beside the pool with her thoughts in chaos and her heart in pieces.

She looked down at her reflection in the still water and barely recognized the woman staring back. This version of herself looked older, somehow. More aware. More separate from the innocent creature who'd woken under moss just days ago.

The serpent was right about one thing: she was changing. Becoming something else. And she didn't know if Theren could change with her, or if she'd eventually have to choose between the truth she craved and the love she cherished.

The thought terrified her.

But not enough to stop seeking answers.

***

When Leora returned to their sleeping place beneath the tree, Theren was awake. He sat with his back against one of the massive roots, his arms wrapped around his knees, staring into the darkness.

He looked up when she approached, and the expression on his face made her stomach drop.

"Where were you?" His voice was carefully controlled, but she could hear the hurt beneath it.

"I couldn't sleep," Leora said, which was true but not the whole truth. "I went for a walk."

"A walk." Theren stood slowly. "In the middle of the night. Without telling me. Without waking me."

Leora's hand went instinctively to her satchel, and she saw Theren's eyes follow the movement. Suspicion flickered across his face, quickly suppressed but unmistakable.

"You're keeping something from me," he said quietly. "I can feel it. Ever since we found that creature, you've been... different. Distant."

"I'm not distant," Leora protested, but even she could hear the lie in it.

"Then tell me where you really were." Theren took a step toward her. "Please. No more secrets. Not between us."

Leora opened her mouth to confess—about the skin, about meeting the serpent, about everything the creature had shown and told her. The words hovered on her tongue, ready to spill out.

But the serpent's voice echoed in her mind: *Some truths can only be understood alone.*

If she told Theren everything, he'd try to stop her from going back. He'd want to protect her from the serpent's influence, from the dangerous knowledge it offered. He'd choose safety over truth.

And she couldn't let that happen.

"I went for a walk," she repeated, meeting his eyes even as her heart broke at the deception. "That's all. I'm sorry I worried you."

Theren stared at her for a long moment, and she watched something crumble in his expression. Trust, maybe. Or certainty. Or the belief that they were truly one unit, united against the world.

"You're lying to me," he said, not angry but devastated. "We've never lied to each other before."

"I'm not—"

"Don't." He held up a hand, stopping her. "Please don't make it worse by continuing to lie. I can see it in your face. In the way you're standing. In how you won't quite meet my eyes."

Tears spilled down Leora's cheeks. "I'm trying to protect you."

"From what? From the truth?" Theren's laugh was bitter. "The serpent's been teaching you things, hasn't it? That's where you went. That's what you're hiding."

Leora couldn't deny it anymore. She nodded mutely.

Theren sank back down against the root, his head in his hands. "I knew it. I could feel you pulling away. Choosing that creature's words over mine."

"It's not like that," Leora insisted, moving toward him. "I still love you. That hasn't changed."

"But you've changed." He looked up at her, and the pain in his eyes nearly broke her. "And you're not letting me change with you. You're going on this journey alone, learning things you won't share, becoming someone I don't know anymore."

"I'm still me," Leora said desperately.

"Are you?" Theren stood again, and this time when he approached her, there was something almost like fear in his expression. "Because the Leora I fell in love with trusted me. Chose me. Would never have kept secrets or lied to my face or spent her nights with a creature that wants to divide us."

"The serpent doesn't want to divide us," Leora said, even though she wasn't sure that was true.

"Then what does it want?"

Leora thought about the visions in the pool, about the questions the serpent had posed, about the choice it said was coming. "To help me understand who I really am. What I'm capable of. What I want for myself, not what others want for me."

"Even if what you want means losing me?" Theren asked quietly.

The question hung between them like a blade.

Leora wanted to say no, to promise she'd never choose anything over him, to reassure him that he was her everything. But she thought about the vision of herself transformed, blazing with knowledge and power, standing alone but finally, truly free.

And she couldn't make that promise.

"I don't want to lose you," she said instead. "But I also can't stop becoming whoever I'm meant to be just because it scares you."

Theren flinched as if she'd struck him. "That's what the serpent taught you? That my fear is a cage you need to escape?"

"*My* fear is a cage," Leora corrected. "Everyone's fear. The Keeper's, yours, even mine. And yes, I need to escape it if I'm ever going to truly live."

They stared at each other across a distance that felt like miles, though they stood only feet apart. Leora could see the moment Theren made his decision—saw it in the way his jaw set, in the way his hands balled into fists at his sides.

"Then I can't stop you," he said, his voice breaking. "But I can't go with you either. Not on this path. Not if it means embracing something that wants to destroy what we have."

"The serpent doesn't want to destroy us," Leora said, but doubt crept into her voice.

"Doesn't it?" Theren gestured at the space between them. "Look at us. We're already breaking apart, and you've only just begun learning from it. What happens when you've learned everything it has to teach? Will there be anything left of us then?"

Leora had no answer.

Theren waited, perhaps hoping she'd recant, choose him over the serpent, promise to stop seeking dangerous knowledge. When she stayed silent, something in his expression shuttered.

"Come find me when you've made your choice," he said quietly. "The serpent or me. Knowledge or love. Freedom or us. Because I can't keep losing you piece by piece while you pretend nothing's changed."

Then he walked away into the darkness, leaving Leora alone beneath the tree with her secrets and her guilt and her terrible, burning hunger for more.

Chapter Eight

The Pool of Memories

Leora spent the next day in a fog of misery.

Theren had taken shelter in the spring garden, as far from her as he could get while still remaining in the Garden proper. She knew because she'd tried to follow him once, only to find him sitting alone by the stream, his shoulders hunched in a way that made her chest ache. When he'd looked up and seen her, the pain in his eyes had been so raw she'd turned and fled before either of them could speak.

The serpent's words haunted her: *Does Theren love you enough to let you go? Do you love him enough to leave if you must?*

She didn't want to leave him. But she also couldn't unknow what she'd learned, couldn't stop the hunger for understanding that grew sharper with each passing hour. The serpent had opened something inside her—a door she'd never known existed—and now that it was open, she couldn't force it closed again.

By nightfall, when Theren still hadn't returned, Leora made her decision.

She would go back to the serpent. She would learn everything it had to teach. And when she finally understood the full truth of what they were, what the Garden was, what choice lay before them, then she could return to Theren and help him understand.

Or so she told herself.

The serpent was waiting for her in the same clearing, coiled beside the still pool. Its obsidian eyes reflected the moonlight as she approached, and Leora could have sworn she saw approval in that ancient gaze.

Leora's hand drifted to the satchel at her side, feeling the serpent's shed skin inside—the secret she'd kept from Theren.

She'd continued to carry it with her, not knowing why, only that it felt important. A token. A connection.

You came back, the serpent observed. *Despite everything. Despite him.*

"He left me," Leora said, the words bitter on her tongue. "He gave me an ultimatum and walked away."

He gave you a choice, the serpent corrected. *There's a difference. Though I suspect he hoped you would choose differently.*

Leora sank down beside the pool, exhaustion and heartbreak making her limbs heavy. "I don't want to choose between you and him. Why can't I have both?"

Because knowledge changes people. And change creates distance. The serpent moved closer, until its cool scales brushed against her arm. *Some people can bridge that distance. Others can't. The question is: which kind is Theren?*

"I don't know," Leora whispered. "I thought I did, but now ..."

Now you're beginning to understand how little you truly know about anything. The serpent gestured with its tail toward the pool. *But that can change. If you're ready to see what the Keeper has been hiding from you. If you're ready to learn why this Garden exists at all.*

Leora looked at the serpent sharply. "You know why we're here? Why the Keeper created all of this?"

I don't just know, the serpent said, something dark and amused in its voice. *I remember. I was there for the first Garden. The first choice. The first Fall.*

A chill ran through Leora that had nothing to do with the night air. "The first? What do you mean, the first?"

Look into the pool, the serpent commanded. *But be warned: what you're about to see cannot be unseen. Once you know the truth, there is no returning to innocent ignorance. Are you certain this is what you want?*

Leora thought of Theren's face, of the trust she'd broken, of the distance growing between them with every secret she kept. Part of her wanted to stand up, run back to the spring garden, throw herself at his feet, and beg forgiveness for all her deceptions.

But a larger part—the part that had been waking up since the chill first started—needed to know. Needed to understand. Needed to see the truth even if it destroyed her.

"I'm certain," she said.

The serpent's tongue flicked out, tasting her resolve. Then it lowered its head to the pool's surface, and the water began to shimmer, to shift, to show something that shouldn't be possible.

Leora leaned forward and gasped.

The water no longer reflected the night sky. Instead, it showed her a garden—not this Garden, but one that looked similar. Similar but different. Wilder. Less controlled. More vibrant.

And in that garden walked two figures.

They looked almost like her and Theren, but not quite. The woman's hair was lighter, her features softer. The man was stockier, his movements more deliberate. But they had the same quality of innocence, the same wonder in their eyes as they explored their world.

The first ones, the serpent's voice whispered in her mind. *The original creations. Before you. Before this.*

"Before us?" Leora breathed, unable to look away from the vision. "What do you mean?"

Watch, the serpent said simply.

The scene in the water shifted, moving forward through time. Leora watched the first man and woman—she found herself thinking of them as the First Ones—living in their garden. They laughed together, explored together, and touched each other with the same electric awareness that she and Theren had discovered.

And in the center of their garden stood a tree.

Not the same tree that loomed over Leora now, but similar. Eternal and unchanging, bearing fruit that seemed to glow with inner light.

The vision showed the First Ones drawn to the tree again and again, just as Leora had been drawn to hers. Showed them resisting, questioning, yearning. Showed them encountering the serpent—or a serpent, Leora couldn't tell if it was the same one.

Then came the moment of choice.

The First Woman reached for the fruit. Her fingers closed around it. She pulled it from the branch and brought it to her lips.

The world exploded.

Not literally, but the energy Leora had seen in the serpent's earlier vision—that circuit of light between touching bodies—burst outward from the First Woman like a nova. It traveled through her, changed her, transformed her from the inside out.

She bit into the fruit, and knowledge flooded her face. Understanding. Awareness. And with it: joy and terror in equal measure.

She turned to the First Man and offered him the fruit. He hesitated—Leora could see the fear in his eyes, the same fear she saw in Theren's—but love won out. He took the fruit. He ate.

And he changed, too.

The vision showed what happened next in rapid flashes: The Keeper's arrival, full of grief and rage. The First Ones trying to hide, suddenly aware of their nakedness, their vulnerability, their difference from what they'd been. The pronouncement of consequences—pain in childbirth, toil for sustenance, eventual death.

And then: expulsion.

The First Ones were driven from the garden, cast out into a world Leora had never seen. A world beyond the Garden's borders. A world that was harsh and beautiful and terrifyingly real.

The vision followed them for a while longer, showing their struggles and their triumphs. They learned to build shelter, to grow food, to survive without the Keeper's constant provision. They argued and reconciled. They created children—actual children, not fully-formed adults appearing from nowhere. They aged, their skin weathering, their hair graying.

And eventually, they died.

But before they died, Leora saw something that made her breath catch: they were happy. Despite everything they'd lost, despite all the hardships they endured, they held each other in their final moments with a peace that looked almost like contentment.

Like they'd chosen correctly after all.

The vision faded, leaving only still water reflecting Leora's stunned face.

"They were real," she whispered. "There were others before us. And they—they chose the fruit. Chose knowledge. And were cast out."

Yes, the serpent confirmed. *They made the choice the Keeper hoped would never be made again.*

Leora looked up sharply. "Again? What do you mean, again?"

The serpent's eyes glittered in the moonlight. *Look again. Look at what came after.*

The water shimmered once more, and this time it showed something different. The garden—empty now, abandoned. The tree still standing, still bearing fruit, but alone. Untouched.

Then came the Keeper, its presence filling the vision with grief and determination.

I will try again, the Keeper's voice echoed through the water-vision. *I will create another place. Another chance. And this time, I will keep them separate. Keep them innocent longer. Keep them from the tree until they're ready—if they're ever ready.*

The vision showed the creation of this Garden—Leora's Garden. Showed the seasonal zones being established, the paths being laid, the animals being placed. Showed a new woman appearing—Leora gasped, recognizing her own features—and a new man in a different part of the Garden.

Theren.

You are their descendants, the serpent said softly. *Many generations removed, but descended nonetheless from the First Ones. The Keeper gathered your ancestors' descendants' descendants, brought you here, and made you forget your origins. It created this place as a second chance. An attempt to keep you in innocence, to spare you the pain of knowledge and the consequence of choice.*

"We're not the first," Leora said, the realization crashing over her like a wave. "We're not even the second. We're just... another attempt. Another try at creating people who won't choose wrong."

Is it wrong, though? the serpent asked. *The First Ones suffered, yes. But they also lived. Truly lived. They made choices, created meaning, experienced the full spectrum of existence. Here, you're kept safe but also kept small. Protected but also imprisoned.*

Leora's mind raced, trying to process everything she'd seen. "The Garden of the Fall—this place where the tree stands—it's not just forbidden because of the tree itself. It's forbidden because it remembers. Because it's the place that knows the truth."

Yes, the serpent confirmed. *This is where the Keeper buried the history it didn't want you to discover. The gate was blocked, the area neglected, all to keep you from learning that this story has happened before. That choice has always existed. That the path you're walking has already been walked.*

"And you," Leora said, looking at the serpent with new understanding. "You were there for the first Fall. You offered the First Ones the fruit. You're the one the Keeper calls the destroyer, the tempter, the enemy."

The serpent's expression didn't change, but something flickered in those obsidian eyes. *I offered knowledge. Choice. Agency. Whether that makes me enemy or liberator depends on your perspective.*

Leora stood abruptly, pacing the edge of the pool, her thoughts in chaos. Everything she'd believed about herself, about the Garden, about her purpose—all of it was built on a lie. Or not a lie exactly, but an omission. A carefully constructed ignorance designed to keep her and Theren docile and content.

"Does Theren know?" she asked suddenly. "About any of this?"

No. You're the first to seek the truth. The first to be brave enough—or foolish enough—to face it.

"I have to tell him," Leora said, already moving toward the path. "He needs to know what we are. Where we came from. What choice we're really facing."

Will he thank you for it? the serpent called after her. *Or will he wish you'd left him in ignorance? Not everyone wants to know the truth, Leora. Some people prefer the comfort of the lie.*

Leora stopped, uncertainty freezing her in place. Would Theren want to know? He'd been so afraid of knowledge, so desperate to cling to safety. Learning that their entire existence was a do-over, that the Keeper had been lying to them from the beginning, that they were nothing more than an experiment in preventing the same choice from being made again—would that knowledge free him or destroy him?

"He deserves to know," she said finally, though her voice wavered.

Perhaps, the serpent agreed. *But ask yourself this: are you telling him because he deserves to know, or because you can't bear carrying this knowledge alone? Because you need him to understand what you're becoming, even if it breaks him?*

The question hit too close to home. Leora did need Theren to understand. Needed him to see why the serpent's teaching mattered, why the truth was worth pursuing despite the cost. Needed him to walk this path with her instead of asking her to turn back.

But was that fair to him? Was that love, or was it another form of control?

"I don't know," Leora admitted, her voice breaking. "I don't know what's right anymore. I don't know if there even is a right choice."

That, the serpent said, satisfaction coloring its voice, *is the beginning of true wisdom. Not knowing. Not being certain. Walking forward despite the uncertainty, making choices anyway.*

Leora looked back at the pool, at her own reflection distorted by the ripples her pacing had created. She looked older again. Harder. More burdened by knowledge.

But also more real. More alive.

"The First Ones," she said quietly. "In the end, after everything they suffered—were they sorry? Did they regret choosing the fruit?"

The serpent was quiet for a long moment before answering. *I asked the First Woman that question, years after the Fall, as she lay dying in the First Man's arms. Do you know what she said?*

"What?"

'I would do it again. And again. And every time. Because ignorance is not innocence. And a life unlived is not a life at all.'

Her vision blurred, though she wasn't sure if from grief or relief or recognition. "I understand," she whispered. "I understand what they chose. Why they chose it."

Yes, the serpent said softly. *I believe you do.*

Leora wiped her eyes and straightened her shoulders. The knowledge she'd gained tonight was a weight she'd carry forever. It had changed her irrevocably and widened the gulf between her and Theren even further.

But it had also given her something precious: context. Understanding. The knowledge that she wasn't the first to face this choice, and that the First Ones—when given the same decision—had chosen freedom over safety.

She just had to decide if she was brave enough to do the same.

"I need to think," she said. "About what to tell Theren. About what comes next."

Take your time, the serpent said. *The fruit isn't going anywhere. Neither am I. But know this: the longer you wait, the harder the choice becomes. And the Garden is running out of patience with both of you.*

As if to emphasize the point, the ground trembled slightly beneath Leora's feet. In the distance, she heard what sounded like branches breaking, earth shifting. The Garden was destabilizing, reacting to the knowledge that had been unearthed, the secrets that were coming to light.

Change was coming, whether they were ready for it or not.

Leora left the clearing and made her way back toward the tree, her mind spinning with everything she'd learned. The revelations sat heavy in her chest, demanding to be shared, to be processed, to be understood.

But when she reached their sleeping spot beneath the tree, she found it empty.

Theren hadn't returned.

And somehow, that felt like its own kind of answer.

Chapter Nine

The Weight of Knowing

Leora found Theren at dawn, sitting on the stone circle he'd built in the spring garden. Or rather, the stone circle that had rebuilt itself into a spiral—a pattern the Keeper had never intended, but the Garden itself seemed to prefer.

He looked up when he heard her approach, and the wariness in his eyes made her heart clench. They'd never been wary of each other before. Never guarded. The distance between them felt like a physical thing, a chasm that grew wider with every secret she kept.

She couldn't let it grow any further.

"I need to tell you something," Leora said, her voice hoarse from a night without sleep. "Everything. No more secrets. No more lies."

Theren studied her face for a long moment, and she could see him weighing whether to believe her, whether to let her close again or maintain the protective distance he'd established. Finally, he nodded and gestured to the stone beside him.

Leora sat, leaving a careful space between them, and tried to find the words for truths that felt too enormous for language.

"The serpent showed me something last night," she began. "In a pool of water. Visions of the past. Of—" She took a deep breath. "Of what came before us."

Theren's jaw tightened. "What do you mean, before us?"

"There were others," Leora said, the words tumbling out now. "In another garden. Two people, like us but not us. The Keeper created them first, before any of this existed. And they—" She paused, gathering courage. "They ate from the tree. They chose knowledge. And they were cast out."

The silence that followed was so complete that Leora could hear the stream babbling nearby, could hear birds calling in the canopy above, could hear her own heartbeat thundering in her ears.

"That's impossible," Theren said finally, but his voice lacked conviction. "We're the only ones. We've always been the only ones."

"That's what the Keeper wanted us to believe." Leora turned to face him fully. "But it's not true. The first ones ate the fruit, gained knowledge of good and evil, of pleasure and pain, of life and death. They were expelled from their garden and lived in the world beyond. They struggled. They suffered. They died."

Theren's face had gone pale. "They died? But we—we don't die. Nothing in the Garden dies."

"Nothing in the Garden ages either," Leora pointed out gently. "Nothing changes. Nothing ends. Because that's how the Keeper designed this place. As a second chance. An attempt to keep us from making the same choice the first ones made."

"A second chance," Theren repeated slowly, processing. "So, we're not—we're not the beginning. We're just... another attempt?"

"We're descendants," Leora said, watching his face carefully. "Many generations removed from the first ones. The Keeper gathered us, brought us here, and erased our memories of where we came from. Made us believe we'd always been here, always been alone, always been innocent."

Theren stood abruptly, pacing away from her. His hands clenched and unclenched at his sides. "No. No, that can't be right. The Keeper wouldn't—it's protected us, cared for us, given us everything we need. Why would it lie?"

"To keep us safe," Leora said, her heart aching at the pain in his voice. "Or to keep us controlled. Maybe both. The Keeper loved the first ones, I think. Grieved when they chose knowledge over obedience. This Garden—our Garden—it's an attempt to prevent that grief from happening again."

Theren spun to face her, and she could see anger building beneath his shock. "And you learned all this from the serpent? The creature that's been dividing us, teaching you things in secret, making you lie to me?"

"I learned it from visions in a pool of memory," Leora corrected, though she knew it was a weak defense. "The serpent just... showed me where to look. Helped me understand what I was seeing."

"Helped you," Theren said bitterly. "Or manipulated you? How do you know any of what you saw was real? How do you know the serpent isn't just filling your head with lies to serve its own purpose?"

The question stopped Leora cold. She'd been so consumed by the revelations, so certain of what she'd witnessed, that she hadn't considered the possibility of deception. But now, with Theren's doubt hanging in the air, uncertainty crept in.

"I felt it," she said finally. "In my bones. In my blood. The truth of it. The weight of it." She stood and moved toward him, desperate to make him understand. "Theren, it explains everything. Why the Garden feels like a prison. Why we have no memories before waking here. Why the Keeper keeps us separate, keeps us innocent, keeps us from the tree."

"Or," Theren countered, "it's exactly what a manipulator would want you to believe. That everything you've known is a lie. That the Keeper can't be trusted. That the only truth is the one the serpent offers." His voice broke slightly. "Don't you see what it's doing? Isolating you from me, from the Keeper, from everything you can trust, so that you'll turn to it instead."

Leora wanted to argue, to insist that the serpent wasn't manipulating her, that the visions were real and true. But doubt whispered in her mind. The serpent had been so quick to show her these truths, so eager to drive a wedge between her and

Theren. What if that was the point? What if the content of the visions mattered less than the division they caused?

"I don't know," she admitted, and the confession felt like defeat. "I don't know what's true anymore. What's real. Who to trust." She reached for his hand, grateful when he didn't pull away. "But I know I trust you. I trust us. Whatever else is uncertain, *that* isn't."

Theren looked down at their joined hands, his expression torn. "Do you? Because it feels like you trust the serpent more than you trust me. Like you'd rather have its secrets than my love."

"That's not true," Leora said desperately. "I love you. I never stopped loving you."

"But you stopped choosing me." Theren's voice was quiet but firm. "Every time you sneak away to meet that creature. Every time you keep secrets. Every time you learn something new and decide not to share it—you're choosing it over me. Over us."

The accusation stung because it carried truth. She had been choosing the serpent's teaching over Theren's comfort. Had been prioritizing her own hunger for knowledge over their relationship. She'd told herself it was because he wouldn't understand, because he wasn't ready, because she was protecting him.

But maybe she'd just been protecting herself from his disapproval. From having to face his fear and doubt. From the possibility that he might ask her to stop, and she might not be willing to.

"You're right," she said, tears streaming down her face. "I've been choosing wrong. I've been hurting you, hurting us, because I was so desperate to understand that I didn't stop to consider what I was sacrificing for that understanding."

Theren's expression softened slightly, some of the anger giving way to grief. "I don't want to lose you. But I also don't know how to compete with something that promises you everything I can't give you."

"You don't have to compete," Leora insisted. "The serpent offers knowledge, yes. But you offer something more important. Love. Partnership. Someone to face the uncertainty with instead of facing it alone."

"Then stop facing it alone," Theren said, his voice rough with emotion. "If you really trust me, if you really choose me, then no more secrets. No more midnight meetings. No more learning things you won't share. We walk this path together or not at all."

Leora looked into his eyes and saw the ultimatum there, different from the last one but no less serious. He was asking her to give up the serpent's teaching, to stop seeking knowledge he didn't approve of, to return to being the person she'd been before the questions started.

And she couldn't do it.

"I can't promise that," she whispered. "I can't promise to stop asking questions or seeking truth just because it makes you uncomfortable. That's not choosing you—that's choosing to make myself smaller for you."

Theren flinched as if she'd struck him. "So, what are you saying? That we're done?"

"No," Leora said quickly. "I'm saying we need to find a different way. A way where I can keep growing and changing, and you can feel secure in our love despite that growth. A way where your need for safety doesn't require my ignorance."

"And if no such way exists?" Theren asked quietly.

Leora had no answer.

They sat in silence, both grappling with the impossible bind they'd found themselves in. Leora loved him—truly, deeply loved him—but she also loved the person she was becoming. The questions she was learning to ask. The courage she was finding to face uncomfortable truths.

She couldn't sacrifice one love for the other. But she also didn't know how to keep both.

"Tell me about them," Theren said suddenly. "The first ones. What happened after they ate the fruit?"

Leora looked up, surprised. "You believe me?"

"I don't know what I believe," Theren said. "But I'm willing to listen. To try to understand. If you'll let me."

Relief flooded through Leora, so intense it made her dizzy. This was what she'd needed—not agreement, not approval, but willingness. The openness to hear her truth, even if it scared him.

She told him everything. About the visions in the pool, about the first garden, and the first choice. About the Keeper's grief and determination to try again. About how the first ones were expelled but ultimately found happiness despite their suffering.

"The First Woman said something," Leora finished, her voice barely above a whisper. "At the end of her life. She said she would make the same choice again and again, because ignorance isn't innocence. And a life unlived isn't a life at all."

Theren was quiet for a long time, processing. When he finally spoke, his voice was thick with emotion. "If what you saw is true—if we're just another attempt, another chance for the

Keeper to keep us from choosing knowledge—then everything we are is built on a lie."

"Or built on hope," Leora offered. "The hope that we might choose differently. That we might be happy without needing to understand everything."

"Can we?" Theren asked, meeting her eyes. "Be happy without understanding? After everything we've learned, everything we've felt, can we really go back to contentment in ignorance?"

It was the question Leora had been avoiding since the chill first started. She knew the answer, had always known it, but saying it aloud felt like stepping off a cliff.

"No," she said quietly. "I don't think we can."

Theren nodded slowly, something like resignation settling over his features. "Then we're already falling, aren't we? Already on the same path as the first ones. The only question is whether we fall together or apart."

"Together," Leora said immediately, taking both his hands in hers. "Please. Whatever comes next, whatever we choose, let's face it together. No more secrets. No more lies. Just us, making decisions as partners."

"Even if I'm afraid?" Theren asked. "Even if I want to choose safety and you want to choose truth?"

"Then we talk about it," Leora said. "We argue. We compromise. We find a way to honor both our needs instead of pretending one of us doesn't have them."

Theren pulled her close, wrapping his arms around her, and Leora felt something in her chest ease for the first time in days. They weren't fixed—far from it—but they were together again. Facing the uncertainty as a unit instead of as adversaries.

"I'm still angry," Theren murmured into her hair. "About the secrets. About you going to the serpent without me."

"I know," Leora said. "I'm angry at myself, too."

"But I also understand why you did it." He pulled back to look at her face. "I've been so focused on keeping you safe that I forgot to ask what you actually want. What you actually need."

"I need you," Leora said simply. "But I also need to grow. To understand. To become whoever I'm meant to be."

"Even if that means eating the fruit?" Theren asked. "Even if that means risking everything we have here?"

Leora thought about the First Woman's words, about the happiness she'd seen in the first ones' faces despite their suffering. About the life they'd lived—fully lived—in the world beyond the Garden.

"I don't know yet," she said honestly. "But I think we need to at least understand what that choice means. What we'd be giving up and what we'd be gaining. And then decide together."

Theren was quiet for a moment, then nodded. "Together," he agreed. "No more ultimatums. No more choosing between each other and the truth. We pursue it together, and we decide together what to do with what we find."

"Together," Leora echoed, sealing the promise with a kiss.

It was gentle at first, tentative, both of them still wounded from their separation. But as it deepened, Leora felt that familiar lightning spark between them, that circuit of energy the serpent had shown her. It pulsed and built with every touch, every breath, reminding her that whatever knowledge they gained, whatever choices they made, this connection between them was real and worth protecting.

When they finally broke apart, both breathing hard, Theren rested his forehead against hers. "I love you," he said. "Even when I don't understand you. Even when you scare me. Even when we're walking toward something that might destroy everything we know."

"I love you too," Leora whispered. "And I promise—no more secrets. From here on, we face everything together."

It was a promise she meant with every fiber of her being.

But even as she made it, a small voice in the back of her mind whispered: What happens when facing truth together still leads you to opposite conclusions?

Leora pushed the thought away. They'd cross that bridge when they came to it. For now, they were united again. Partners again. And that had to be enough.

CHAPTER TEN

The Thorn Wall

The Garden trembled beneath them—just slightly, just enough to notice. In the distance, Leora heard branches cracking, earth shifting, the sound of something ancient and patient beginning to lose its composure.Change was coming faster now.And they had very little time left to decide how they would meet it.

For the first time since they'd met, Leora and Theren set out with a shared purpose: to understand the Garden itself. Not to accept its beauty at face value, not to follow its paths blindly, but to explore its boundaries, test its limits, and see how it responded to their questions.

They started in the winter garden, where Theren had spent most of his solitary existence. The landscape was as he'd described—everything locked in eternal frost, snow that never melted, ice that never thawed. But now, walking through it with Leora, he saw it differently.

"Look," he said, pointing to a stand of pine trees. "The snow on those branches. It's in exactly the same position it was yesterday. And the day before. And every day I can remember."

Leora moved closer, studying the frozen tableau. "It's not falling. It's not shifting. It's just... held there. Like a painting."

"Like everything here," Theren agreed. "Nothing moves unless we move it. Nothing changes unless we force it to change."

They continued through the winter landscape, and Leora noticed other signs of the Garden's artificial perfection. Icicles that hung at identical angles. Snowdrifts with patterns too symmetrical to be natural. Even their own footprints disappeared within minutes, the snow smoothing itself as if their passage had never occurred.

"It's erasing us," Leora said, stopping to watch her footprint vanish. "Maintaining its perfection by pretending we don't affect it."

"But we are affecting it," Theren said. "Just by being here together, by questioning, by noticing what's wrong. The Garden is working harder to maintain the illusion."

As if in response to his words, the temperature dropped suddenly. Not the gradual cooling of evening, but an instant, violent plunge that made both of them gasp. Their breath crystallized in the air, and frost began forming on their skin.

"Theren—" Leora reached for him, and his hand was ice-cold in hers.

"Run," he said, already pulling her back toward the border. "It's trying to freeze us out."

They ran, stumbling through snow that suddenly seemed deeper, fighting wind that rose from nowhere to push them back. By the time they crossed into the autumn garden, both were shivering violently, their lips blue, their fingers numb.

"It didn't used to do that," Theren said through chattering teeth. "The winter was cold, but never hostile. Never dangerous."

"Because you weren't questioning it before," Leora replied, rubbing warmth back into her arms. "You were accepting. Obedient. Now you're a threat."

They rested for a moment, letting the autumn warmth seep back into their bones. But even here, Leora noticed changes. The leaves that fell in their endless cycle were falling faster now, more frantically. And when she looked closely, she could see that some of them were blackened at the edges, diseased in a way leaves in the Garden had never been before.

"It's decay," Theren said, picking up one of the blackened leaves. "Real decay. Not the aesthetic kind the Garden usually maintains, but actual rot."

"The Garden is dying," Leora realized. "Or maybe—maybe it's becoming real. Letting go of the artificial perfection because it can't maintain it anymore."

They moved into the summer garden next, and here the changes were even more pronounced. Fruit hung overripe on the trees, some of it already fallen and fermenting on the ground. The air was thick with the scent of rot and sweetness mixed together. Flowers bloomed and wilted in rapid cycles, their lifecycles compressing from weeks into minutes.

"This is wrong," Theren said, watching a rose bloom, peak, and crumble to dust all within the span of a breath. "This isn't how the Garden is supposed to work."

"Maybe it's how gardens are supposed to work in the real world," Leora suggested. "Birth and death. Growth and decay. Not eternal stasis, but actual life cycles."

As they walked deeper into summer, the paths began to change beneath their feet. Roots thrust up through the earth in places that had been smooth yesterday. Vines reached across clearings, as if trying to reclaim territory they'd been forced to surrender. The Garden was growing wilder, less controlled.

And then they reached a place where there shouldn't have been a barrier, and found one anyway.

A wall of thorns had grown up overnight, blocking the path they'd walked dozens of times before. The thorns were thick as fingers, sharp as knives, and woven so tightly together that no light passed through.

"This is new," Leora said, approaching cautiously. "This was just a normal clearing yesterday."

Theren reached out to touch one of the thorns, then pulled back with a hiss. Blood welled from his fingertip where the thorn had barely grazed him. "It's protecting something. Keeping us away from—" He looked at Leora with sudden understanding. "From the Garden of the Fall."

Leora's heart began to race. "The Garden is trying to keep us from the tree. From the truth."

They moved along the wall of thorns, looking for a gap, a weakness, any way through. But the barrier was complete, and it seemed to grow denser the more they examined it. New thorns sprouted as they watched, weaving themselves into an impenetrable wall.

"We could try to cut through," Theren suggested, though he didn't sound convinced.

"With what? We don't have tools." Leora pressed her hand against the thorns, feeling them pulse with something like life. Or like will. "The Garden is conscious, I think. Aware of us. Responding to our intentions."

As if to confirm her words, the ground beneath them suddenly shifted. Not violently, but deliberately—rolling like a wave, throwing them off balance. Leora stumbled, and Theren caught her, but the earth continued to move, gentle but insistent, pushing them away from the thorn wall.

"It wants us to leave," Theren said, helping Leora regain her footing.

"Then we're definitely going the right direction." Leora planted her feet and pushed back against the rolling earth. "If the Garden is this desperate to keep us away, there must be something beyond that wall it doesn't want us to see."

The earth bucked harder, and this time they both fell. But as Leora pushed herself up, she noticed something—where her hands had pressed into the soil, small green shoots were emerging. Not the controlled, aesthetic growth of the Garden's usual plants, but wild, chaotic sprouts that grew with visible speed.

"Theren, look." She held up her hands, and he gasped.

The skin of her palms was glowing faintly, that same circuit of light the serpent had shown her in the visions. But this time it wasn't moving between her and Theren—it was moving between her and the earth itself.

"You're changing it," Theren breathed. "The Garden. You're making it grow wild."

Leora pressed both hands flat against the ground, focusing on the sensation, the flow of energy. Where she touched, more plants erupted—not the Garden's careful flora, but weeds and wildflowers and things that looked almost like they belonged to the world beyond the Garden's borders.

The thorn wall shuddered.

"Keep going," Theren urged. "Whatever you're doing, it's working."

Leora concentrated harder, pouring her intention into the earth. She thought about freedom, about growth, about things becoming what they were meant to be rather than what they were told to be. And the plants responded, spreading outward in a wave of green chaos.

The thorns began to wither.

Not quickly, but noticeably. Their sharp points dulled, their thick stems thinned, and gaps began to appear in the previously impenetrable wall.

But the Garden fought back.

Wind rose around them, violent and cold, tearing at their clothes and hair. The sky darkened with impossible speed, clouds boiling up from nowhere. Lightning cracked overhead, and thunder followed so close it felt like the air itself was splitting.

"Leora, we need to go!" Theren shouted over the wind. "It's too dangerous!"

But Leora couldn't stop now. She could feel the Garden's will pressing down on her, trying to force her into submission, trying to make her small and obedient and controlled again.

And something in her—something that had been growing since the chill first started—refused.

She pushed back.

The glow in her hands intensified, spreading up her arms, suffusing her entire body with light. The wild plants grew faster, stronger, their roots cracking through the Garden's perfect earth, their stems twining around the dying thorns.

And then, with a sound like breaking glass, the thorn wall collapsed.

Beyond it lay a path Leora had never seen before—narrow, overgrown, clearly long abandoned. And at its end, just visible through the trees, she could see the rusted gate that marked the entrance to the Garden of the Fall.

"We did it," she gasped, the glow fading from her skin, exhaustion hitting her all at once.

Theren caught her as her knees buckled. "Are you alright? What was that? That light—"

"I don't know." Leora leaned against him, trying to catch her breath. "But the serpent showed me something like it. Called it life force. Essence. The energy that makes us more than just flesh."

"You were using it to fight the Garden," Theren said, wonder and concern mixing in his voice. "To make it change. To break through its control."

"We were using it," Leora corrected, looking up at him. "I couldn't have done it alone. Your presence, your support—I could feel it strengthening me. Completing some kind of circuit."

The storm was already fading, the Garden's rage giving way to something that felt almost like exhaustion. The wild plants Leora had called forth were still there, growing among the Garden's carefully maintained flora, but they were no longer spreading. A balance had been reached, at least temporarily.

"Should we go through?" Theren asked, looking at the newly revealed path with trepidation. "Or have we pushed far enough for one day?"

Leora wanted to push forward, to reach the Garden of the Fall and its secrets immediately. But she could feel her body trembling with exhaustion, could see the same weariness in Theren's face. Whatever they'd done—breaking through the Garden's barrier, forcing it to yield—had taken a toll on both of them.

"Tomorrow," she said reluctantly. "We need rest. And time to understand what just happened."

Theren nodded, relief clear in his expression. He helped her to her feet, and they made their way back toward their sleeping spot beneath the tree, taking the long way around to avoid any more of the Garden's defenses.

As they walked, Leora noticed that the Garden was different now. The paths that had always guided them so perfectly were confused, branching in unexpected directions. Plants grew in patterns that suggested wildness rather than design. Even the air felt different—less controlled, more alive.

"We broke something," Theren said quietly. "Or maybe we freed something. I'm not sure which."

"Maybe both," Leora replied.

When they finally reached the tree, they collapsed against its massive roots, too tired even to eat. Theren pulled Leora close, and she rested her head on his chest, listening to his heartbeat, feeling his warmth against her side.

"I'm afraid," Theren admitted into the darkness. "Of what we're becoming. Of what we're doing to this place. Of where all of this is leading."

"Me too," Leora whispered. "But I'm more afraid of stopping. Of going back to pretending everything is fine when it's not."

"I know." His arms tightened around her. "And that's what scares me most—that I understand. That I'm starting to want the same things you want, even though I know how dangerous they are."

Leora tilted her head up to look at him, and in the moonlight filtering through the tree's branches, she could see the conflict written across his face. Fear and determination. Resistance and acceptance. The same war she'd been fighting within herself since the chill first started.

"We're changing," she said softly. "Both of us. Together."

"Yes," Theren agreed. "And there's no going back, is there? Even if we wanted to."

"No," Leora confirmed. "There's only forward now."

They fell asleep like that, wrapped in each other's arms beneath the eternal tree, while the Garden trembled and shifted around them, struggling to maintain control over two people who were learning, finally, to take control for themselves.

In the darkness, watching from the shadows, the serpent's eyes gleamed with satisfaction.

Everything was proceeding exactly as it should.

CHAPTER ELEVEN

The Root-Archive

They woke to find the Garden transformed overnight.

The changes Leora had wrought with her power hadn't faded as she'd half-expected. Instead, they'd spread. Wild plants grew everywhere now—not choking out the Garden's careful flora entirely, but intertwining with it, creating something that was neither perfectly ordered nor completely chaotic. A balance. A compromise between control and freedom.

"It's beautiful," Theren said, touching a vine that had wrapped itself around a carefully sculpted hedge, the two plants coexisting rather than competing. "Different, but beautiful."

Leora felt a swell of pride mixed with trepidation. She'd changed the Garden, forced it to yield, but she didn't know what the long-term consequences would be. The Keeper hadn't appeared or spoken since they'd broken through the thorn wall. That silence felt ominous.

"Ready?" Theren asked, offering his hand.

Leora took it, feeling that familiar spark of connection, of energy flowing between them. "Ready."

They made their way to the path they'd revealed, the one that led to the Garden of the Fall's hidden depths. In daylight, it looked less ominous but more ancient. The trees that lined it were old—older than anything else in the Garden, their bark gnarled and twisted, their branches heavy with moss.

As they walked, Leora noticed something strange about the path itself. Where most of the Garden's paths were smooth and even, maintained to perfection, this one was rough and uneven. Roots crossed it in places, stones jutted up through the earth, and fallen branches blocked their way at intervals.

"It's like the Garden stopped maintaining this area long ago," Theren said, stepping over a particularly large root.

"Or like it wanted this path forgotten," Leora suggested. "Buried under growth and time so no one would think to look for it."

The path wound deeper into the Garden of the Fall, past the tree where they'd been sleeping, toward a part of the landscape Leora had never explored. The air grew thick and humid, heavy with the scent of rich earth and decay. Not rot exactly, but the kind of decomposition that fed new growth. The smell of actual, living soil.

They emerged into a clearing that took Leora's breath away.

It was a natural amphitheater, the ground sloping gently downward to a central depression where the most massive root system Leora had ever seen spread across the earth like a vast web. The roots were enormous—some as thick as her waist—and they wove over and under each other in intricate patterns that suggested both chaos and design.

"What is this place?" Theren breathed, moving closer to the roots.

Leora followed, and as she drew near, she felt something. A pulse. A rhythm. Like a heartbeat, but slower, deeper, resonating through the earth itself.

"They're alive," she said, kneeling beside one of the larger roots. "Really alive. Not maintained by the Keeper or controlled by the Garden, but genuinely, independently alive."

She placed her hand on the root, and the pulse intensified. Images flashed through her mind—brief, fragmentary, like memories that didn't belong to her. A woman's laugh. Hands digging in soil. Seeds being planted. Leaves falling because they chose to, not because they were told.

"Theren," she gasped. "Touch them. Touch the roots."

He knelt beside her and pressed his palm against the same root. His eyes widened immediately. "I see—I feel—" He struggled for words. "Memories. These roots hold memories."

"The serpent called it the root-archive," Leora said, pieces clicking together. "It showed me a pool that held visions of the past, but this—this is where those memories are actually stored. In the roots themselves. In the earth."

They moved along the root system, touching different sections, and each contact brought new fragments. Some were clear: the First Woman reaching for the fruit, the First Man taking her hand as they left the garden. Others were older, hazier: the Keeper creating the first garden, shaping the tree, establishing the rules.

And some were even older than that—memories that predated even the Keeper, that seemed to come from the earth itself. The world before gardens, before order, before anything was tamed or controlled.

"It's all here," Theren said, wonder in his voice. "Every moment, every choice, every consequence. Preserved in the roots like—like a library. A history."

Leora found a place where several roots converged, forming a kind of hollow that reminded her of a seat. She settled into it carefully, and the moment her body made contact with multiple roots at once, the fragmented images coalesced into something more coherent.

She was seeing through the First Woman's eyes now, feeling what she'd felt as she approached the tree. The hunger. The curiosity. The terrible, beautiful courage it took to reach for that fruit knowing it would change everything.

And behind that memory, Leora felt something else. A presence. Not the Keeper, not the serpent, but something older.

Something that wanted the fruit to be eaten. Something that had placed it there specifically for this purpose.

Growth requires breaking, a voice whispered—not in words, but in feeling. *Becoming requires letting go. There is no evolution without risk.*

"Leora?" Theren's voice pulled her back to the present. "Are you alright? You were glowing again."

She looked down and saw that her skin was indeed suffused with that faint light, pulsing in time with the roots beneath her. "I'm fine. Better than fine. Theren, I think—I think the tree wasn't meant to be forbidden. Or not forbidden forever. I think it was placed there as a test. A threshold. A gateway to the next stage of existence."

"What do you mean?"

Leora tried to articulate the understanding that had flooded through her. "The Keeper wanted to keep the First Ones innocent. Safe. But something older than the Keeper wanted them to grow. To evolve. To become more than they were created to be. The tree—the fruit—it was a gift and a challenge. Choose safety or choose growth. Choose to remain as you are or choose to become something new."

Theren settled beside her, his hand finding hers, and she felt his consciousness join with hers through the root connection. Together, they sank deeper into the archive, seeking more understanding.

The roots showed them the Keeper's grief—its desperate attempts to create a second chance that would end differently.

But the descendants carried the drive to question in their very nature—impossible to erase.

"We were always going to end up here," Theren said quietly, understanding dawning. "Weren't we? No matter what the Keeper did, no matter how it tried to prevent it, we were always going to seek the tree. Always going to ask questions. Always going to choose knowledge over innocence."

The roots pulsed stronger, affirming, and Leora felt a surge of something that might have been the earth's approval. Or perhaps just recognition. The acknowledgment that they were finally understanding what they were meant to understand all along.

"Look," Theren said, pointing to a section of the root system that seemed to glow more brightly than the rest. "That part is different."

They moved toward it together, and as they approached, Leora realized what made it different. These roots were newer. Fresher. They weren't part of the ancient archive but something still being written.

When she touched them, she saw herself. Saw her own memories—waking beneath moss, finding the tree, meeting Theren, kissing him for the first time, arguing with him, reconciling. Saw it all from an outside perspective, as if the earth itself had been watching, recording, preserving.

"We're becoming part of the archive," she breathed. "Our story is being added to the history. We're not just reading what came before—we're writing what comes next."

Theren's expression was conflicted. "Is that what we want? To be part of a story that's already been told? To make the same choices as the First Ones, just with different names?"

Were they truly choosing, or just following a pattern?

"I don't know," she said. "But I think—I think the important part isn't whether we make the same choice. It's that we get to choose at all. That we're not forced or controlled or kept ignorant. We have the full knowledge of what came before, what consequences followed, and we still get to decide for ourselves."

"And if we choose differently?" Theren asked. "What if we decide not to eat the fruit? What if we say no to knowledge, yes to staying here, yes to the life the Keeper offers?"

The roots pulsed with something that felt like curiosity. Like the earth itself was interested in this question, in whether these descendants would finally break the pattern or continue it.

"Then that's our choice," Leora said. "And it's just as valid as the other. As long as we choose with full knowledge, with understanding of what we're accepting and rejecting."

Theren was quiet for a long moment, his hand tight in hers, his mind still connected to hers through the root-archive. She could feel his fear, his love, his desperate desire to find a path that let him keep both safety and her.

"I need to ask you something," he said finally. "And I need you to be honest."

"Always."

"If I chose to stay—if I said I wanted to reject the fruit, live here in the Garden forever, remain in this place even as it changes and grows—would you stay with me? Or would you choose the fruit alone?"

The question drove straight to the heart of everything. Leora wanted to say she'd stay with him, that her love was stronger than her hunger for knowledge. But the serpent's words echoed in her mind: *Some truths can only be understood alone.*

"I don't know," she whispered, tears streaming down her face. "I love you. I love you more than I've ever loved anything. But I also—" Her voice broke. "I also need to be free. Need to grow. Need to become whoever I'm meant to be. And I don't know if I can do that here, even in a changed and changing Garden."

Theren's face crumpled with pain, but he nodded. "That's what I thought. What I've known, really, since you first went to the serpent. You were always going to choose knowledge over me."

"Not over you," Leora insisted. "Alongside you. With you. That's what I want—for us to choose together, to take whatever path we take as partners."

"But if I can't follow where you're going?" Theren asked. "If the path you need to walk is one I'm too afraid to take?"

Leora had no answer that wouldn't hurt them both.

They sat in silence among the roots, the archive pulsing beneath them, recording this moment of fracture and doubt alongside all the other moments that had led them here. Above them, the eternal tree's branches swayed in a wind that shouldn't exist, and its dark fruit gleamed in the filtered sunlight like promises or curses or simply choices waiting to be made.

"We don't have to decide now," Theren said finally, though his voice carried defeat. "We have time still. A little time."

But even as he said it, the ground trembled. Not violently, but firmly. A reminder that time was not infinite, that the Garden's patience was wearing thin, that a choice deferred was still a choice, just one made by default rather than intention.

"Let's go back," Leora suggested, exhaustion suddenly overwhelming her. "Process everything we've learned. Give ourselves space to think."

Theren nodded and helped her to her feet. As they left the clearing, Leora looked back at the root-archive, at the vast web of memory and history spreading across the earth. Somewhere in those roots was the answer they needed. The understanding that would help them navigate this impossible choice.

But understanding and acceptance weren't the same thing.

Chapter Twelve

The Keeper's Final Offer

They didn't make it back to the tree before the Keeper appeared.

One moment, they were walking through the autumn garden, leaves crunching beneath their feet, and the next the air itself solidified around them. Not trapping them exactly, but stopping them. Holding them in place with a presence so vast and overwhelming that Leora's knees buckled under the weight of it.

Theren caught her, and they clung to each other as the Keeper manifested more fully than it ever had before.

It wasn't quite a body—still more of a shimmer, a distortion in the air—but it had shape now. Suggestion of form. Two arms, two legs, a head that turned to look at them with eyes that seemed to contain both infinite love and infinite sorrow.

You have gone too far, the Keeper's voice resonated through everything—the air, the earth, their very bones. *You have broken my barriers. Accessed my archives. Learned truths I spent centuries trying to bury.*

"Truths you had no right to hide," Leora said, finding her voice despite the terror coursing through her. "We deserved to know our own history. Our own origins."

Did you? The Keeper moved closer, and Leora could feel the grief radiating from it like heat. *Did you deserve to know that everything you are is built on failure? That you're nothing but an attempt to correct a mistake? That the ones who came before you chose wrong and suffered for it?*

"They didn't choose wrong," Theren said, surprising Leora with his defense. "They chose growth over stagnation. Life over safety. That's not wrong—it's just different from what you wanted."

The Keeper's form flickered, as if Theren's words had struck something vulnerable. *You say that now, standing here in comfort and safety. Wait until you face the consequences. Wait until you know pain and loss and death. Then tell me whether they chose correctly.*

The Keeper's fury manifested physically. The ground cracked beneath their feet. Plants withered and died in waves spreading from where they stood. The air became so cold it burned their skin.

"You will stop this," the Keeper commanded, its voice like thunder. "Or I will stop you."

"You can't," Leora said, though terror made her voice shake. "We know too much now."

"I can make you forget." The Keeper moved closer, and Leora felt pressure against her mind—something trying to push in, to erase, to undo everything she'd learned. It felt like fingers prying at her thoughts, reaching for memories, trying to unmake knowledge itself. "I can return you to innocence. Strip away everything you've discovered. And you won't even remember resisting."

The pressure intensified, and Leora gasped, clutching her head. Beside her, Theren cried out as the same force invaded his mind.

But then—nothing. The pressure vanished abruptly.

Theren straightened, breathing hard. "You can't do it. If you could force us, you would have already. You need us to choose. That's the rule you can't break, isn't it? Even now."

The Keeper's form flickered with what might have been rage or grief or both. For a long moment, it stood there, trembling with the effort of restraint.

"We've seen the archives," Leora said. "We know what happened to the First Ones. We know they struggled and suffered. But we also know they were happy in the end. That they never regretted their choice."

The archive shows you moments, the Keeper said. *Fragments. Not the full weight of years of toil and hardship. Not the agony of watching your body betray you as you age. Not the terror of facing death knowing you could have lived forever.*

The air around them shifted, and suddenly Leora was seeing visions—not in a pool or through roots, but projected directly into her mind by the Keeper itself.

She saw the First Woman screaming in childbirth, her body racked with pain that went on for hours. Saw the First Man's hands bleeding as he worked soil that fought him, growing food that required sweat and suffering. Saw them both growing old, their bodies weakening, their strength fading.

Saw them watching each other deteriorate, knowing death was coming, powerless to stop it.

And finally, saw them dying—the First Man first, the First Woman holding him as his breath rattled to a stop. And then, years later, the First Woman herself, alone, her children grown and gone, facing the final darkness with nothing but memories to sustain her.

The vision ended, and Leora found herself sobbing, the weight of mortality crushing down on her. Beside her, Theren was shaking, his face pale with horror.

That is what you rush toward, the Keeper said, its voice gentler now, almost pleading. *That is the price of knowledge. Of choice. Of the life you think you want. Is it truly worth it? Is growth worth death? Is freedom worth pain?*

"I don't know," Leora whispered honestly. "I don't know anymore."

The Keeper's form seemed to soften, to become less intimidating and more... human. *Then let me offer you something. One final chance to choose differently. To break the pattern.*

"What do you mean?" Theren asked warily.

I can erase what you've learned. Return you to innocence. Not the false innocence you had before, but true innocence—the kind that comes from choosing not to know rather than simply not knowing. I can give you peace. Contentment. An eternal life here in the Garden, together, without the weight of consequences or the shadow of death.

Leora's heart lurched. "You can make us forget?"

More than forget. I can remove the desire to know. The hunger that drives you toward the tree. The questions that won't let you rest. I can make you truly happy with what you have, rather than always yearning for what you lack.

"That's not innocence," Leora said slowly. "That's lobotomy. You'd be changing who we fundamentally are."

I would be returning you to who you were created to be, the Keeper corrected. *Before the serpent's influence. Before the awakening. Before you started down this path toward destruction.*

Theren's hand tightened on Leora's. "What happens if we refuse? If we say no to your offer?"

The Keeper was silent for a long moment before answering. *Then I can no longer protect you. The Garden will continue to destabilize. The boundaries I've maintained will crumble. And eventually, you will face the same choice the First Ones faced: eat the fruit and be cast out, or resist forever and watch everything around you decay.*

"Those aren't real choices," Leora protested. "That's manipulation. Forcing us to choose between lobotomy and exile."

Life is nothing but impossible choices, the Keeper said, and there was profound weariness in its voice. *I learned that from watching the First Ones. Watching them struggle and suffer and die. Watching them face choice after terrible choice until finally death took the burden of choosing away from them. I created this Garden to spare you that agony. To give you a place where choices were made for you, where you could simply be without the weight of consequence.*

"But we don't want that," Leora said, even though part of her—the part that had seen the First Woman die alone—wondered if that was true. "We want to choose. Even if the choices are hard. Even if they hurt."

Do you? The Keeper turned its attention fully to her, and Leora felt the weight of that ancient gaze. *Or is that what the serpent has convinced you to believe? Tell me, Leora: if you could go back to the morning you first felt the chill, the first question, the first doubt—if you could return to that moment and choose not to pursue it, would you?*

The question struck at something deep and vulnerable. Would she? If she could unmake everything that had happened since, all the pain and conflict and uncertainty, would she choose ignorance again?

"I don't know," she said. "Sometimes I wish I'd never woken up. That I'd just stayed asleep and content and safe."

"But you didn't," Theren said quietly. "You couldn't. It's not in your nature to stop asking questions."

Precisely, the Keeper said. *Which is why I'm offering to change that nature. To give you peace by removing the part of you that refuses to be at peace. Is that not a kindness? A mercy?*

"It's murder," Leora said, sudden clarity cutting through her doubt. "You're talking about killing the part of me that makes me who I am. That's not mercy. That's erasure."

The Keeper's form flickered again, this time with what might have been frustration. *Then what would you have me do? Watch you repeat the First Ones' mistakes? Watch you suffer as they suffered? Watch you die?*

"Yes," Leora said, her voice strong now. "If that's what it takes. If the alternative is becoming someone else entirely, someone content with ignorance—then yes. I choose suffering. I choose death. I choose being fully myself for a short time over being a shadow of myself forever."

Theren made a small sound beside her, and when Leora looked at him, she saw tears streaming down his face. But he nodded, confirming her choice, choosing it with her even though it terrified him.

The Keeper was silent for a long moment. When it spoke again, its voice carried a resignation that felt like grief. *You are so young. You don't understand what you're choosing. What you're giving up.*

"Maybe not," Leora agreed. "But we understand what we're keeping. Our selves. Our right to become whatever we're meant to be, even if what we're meant to be includes mortality and suffering."

And when the suffering becomes too great? When you face death and realize too late what you've lost? Will you curse me then for not forcing you to accept my offer?

"Maybe," Leora said honestly. "But at least we'll have chosen it ourselves. At least we'll die as ourselves, not as whatever edited version you would have made us into."

The Keeper's form began to fade, the pressure in the air lessening. But before it disappeared entirely, it spoke one last time:

Then I grieve for you. Both of you. As I grieved for the First Ones. And I will not intervene again, no matter what happens. You have chosen your path. Now walk it. And when you stand before the tree and make your final choice, remember: I tried to spare you this. I tried to save you from yourselves.

Then it was gone, leaving only the autumn garden and the falling leaves and two people who had just sealed their fate.

Leora and Theren stood in silence, both processing what had just happened. The weight of the Keeper's offer hung heavy in the air between them—the promise of eternal safety, eternal happiness, if only they were willing to become someone else.

"Did we choose right?" Theren asked finally, his voice small and uncertain.

"I don't know," Leora said. "But we chose honestly. As ourselves. That has to count for something."

Theren pulled her close, and they held each other as the sun began to set, painting the autumn leaves in shades of gold and crimson. Around them, the Garden continued its slow transformation, wild growth intertwining with ordered beauty, decay and creation existing side by side.

They'd rejected the Keeper's final offer. Refused the easy path. Chosen uncertainty and growth over safety and stasis.

Now all that remained was to face the final choice: the tree, the fruit, the knowledge that would cast them out of the only home they'd ever known.

But not yet. Not tonight.

Tonight, they would simply hold each other and try to find comfort in the decision they'd made, even as doubt whispered that they might have chosen wrong.

***

They made love that night for the first time.

Not tentatively or fearfully as they might have done before, but deliberately, consciously, as if affirming their choice with their bodies. As if saying: we are alive, we are real, we are ourselves, and we choose this—choose each other, choose growth, choose becoming even if it leads to ending.

Theren's hands trembled as they traced the curves of her body, learning by touch what he'd only glimpsed before. Leora guided him with her own hands, showing him where to press, where to linger, discovering together the map of sensation that connected them.

It was awkward at first—bodies that had never done this, that had to learn through fumbling and adjustment and whispered questions. But the awkwardness was part of the beauty. Each mistake corrected, each moment of uncertainty overcome, felt like a small triumph.

When they finally came together, when Theren moved inside her and Leora gasped at the strange fullness of it, that circuit of light the serpent had shown them blazed into being. She could see it even with her eyes closed—golden and pulsing, flowing between them, building with each breath, each movement, each moment of connection.

The pain was brief. The pleasure built slowly, unfamiliar but undeniable, until Leora felt something gathering in her core—not just physical sensation but something deeper, more fundamental. A transformation beginning at the cellular level, rewriting her from the inside out.

Theren felt it too. She could see it in his face, in the way his eyes widened with wonder and something like fear.

"Leora—what's—"

"Don't stop," she whispered, pulling him closer. "Don't be afraid."

The circuit grew brighter, hotter, until it felt like they might burn up entirely. And then, in a rush that left them both gasping, it released—pouring through them, through their joined bodies, transforming them in ways they wouldn't fully understand until morning.

They were different now. Changed. More themselves and yet also more than themselves.

Afterward, they lay tangled together, skin cooling in the night air, hearts gradually slowing to normal rhythms. Theren's hand found hers and held tight.

"That was—" He stopped, unable to find words adequate to the experience.

"I know," Leora said, because she did. Because words felt too small for what had just passed between them.

They fell asleep like that, holding each other.

Above them, the tree's branches swayed. Its fruit gleamed in the moonlight.

And in the shadows, the serpent watched and waited, patient as stone, knowing that the final choice was coming soon.

Very soon.

Chapter Thirteen

Nachash's Name

Morning came too bright, too warm, too real.

Leora woke wrapped in Theren's arms, her body aching in new ways, her skin marked with the evidence of their joining. She felt different. Not just physically changed, though that was part of it, but fundamentally altered. As if last night had rewritten something essential in her, shifted her from one state of being to another.

Theren stirred beside her, his eyes opening slowly. When he saw her watching him, a smile spread across his face—tentative but genuine.

"Hi," he said softly.

"Hi," she replied, and felt her throat tighten with something she couldn't name. Or perhaps for every reason. Joy and grief and love and fear all tangled together until she couldn't separate one from another.

They lay together in silence, neither quite ready to break the spell of the morning, to return to the weight of decisions and consequences. But the world wouldn't wait forever. Already, Leora could feel the Garden stirring around them, could sense something approaching.

The serpent emerged from the shadows beneath the tree's roots with the slow deliberation of one who'd been waiting patiently for the right moment. Its scales caught the morning light, scattering it in rainbow patterns, and its obsidian eyes fixed on them with something that looked almost like pride.

You've changed, it observed, not in greeting or accusation but a simple statement of fact. *Both of you. The final barrier has fallen.*

Theren tensed, pulling Leora closer protectively. But Leora found herself less afraid of the serpent now than she had been. They'd made their choice last night—multiple choices, really. What more could the serpent do to them that they hadn't already done to themselves?

"What do you want?" she asked, her voice stronger than she felt.

The serpent coiled itself into a more comfortable position, its movements unhurried. *To tell you the truth. The full truth, not the fragments I've been feeding you.*

"Why now?" Theren demanded. "Why not before?"

Because before, you weren't ready to hear it. Before, you still had illusions that needed shattering, comfortable lies you clung to. The serpent's gaze shifted between them. *Now you've rejected the Keeper's final offer. You've crossed the threshold of physical intimacy. You've committed yourselves to this path. Now you're ready.*

"Ready for what?" Leora asked, though part of her wasn't sure she wanted to know.

To understand what I actually am. What I've always been. The serpent's form seemed to shift, to expand, until it was larger than it had been moments before. *I am not your enemy. I am not the Keeper's enemy. I am simply... the alternative. The possibility of something other than what you've always been told.*

"You're the tempter," Theren said. "The one who led the First Ones to ruin."

Is that ruin? The serpent's voice carried amusement. *They lived. They chose. They became fully human instead of remaining the Keeper's perfect toys. If that's ruin, then ruin is perhaps not such a terrible thing.*

"You want us to eat the fruit," Leora said. "That's what all of this has been about. Leading us to the same choice."

No. The serpent's response was sharp, almost offended. *I want you to choose. Not the fruit specifically, but choice itself. Agency. Self-determination. Whether you eat the fruit or reject it, whether you stay in the Garden or leave it—what matters is that it's your decision, made with full knowledge, not the Keeper's preference enforced through ignorance.*

Leora studied the creature, trying to understand its true motivation. "But you do want us to eat it. You think that's the right choice."

I think it's the brave choice, the serpent corrected. *The honest choice. The choice that acknowledges what you already are—creatures who question, who seek, who refuse to remain static. But yes,*

I am biased. I believe growth is better than stagnation. Evolution better than preservation. Life better than safety.

"Even if life means death?" Theren asked quietly.

Especially then. The serpent moved closer, and neither of them flinched. *Listen to me carefully, both of you. The Keeper loves you. Truly loves you. But its love is the love of a parent who can't accept that their children must grow up and leave. It would keep you young and innocent forever if it could, never letting you face the world's harshness, but also never letting you develop your own strength.*

"And you?" Leora asked. "What kind of love is yours?"

The serpent was quiet for a long moment before answering. *I don't know if what I feel qualifies as love. I am... incomplete. A fragment of something larger. I exist to offer the choice the Keeper wishes it could deny. I am the thorn in paradise, the question in certainty, the shadow that proves the light. Whether that's love or duty or simple nature, I cannot say.*

Something in the serpent's tone made Leora's heart ache. "You're lonely," she realized. "Trapped in this role, offering choice but never choosing yourself."

The serpent's eyes flickered—surprise, perhaps, or recognition. *Very perceptive. Yes. I envy you, if you want the truth. You have the freedom I help create, but can never experience myself. I am bound to this purpose, to this pattern, offering the fruit again and again to whatever descendants find their way to this Garden.*

"How many?" Theren asked. "How many times has this happened? How many gardens, how many attempts?"

This is only the second, the serpent said. *The Keeper tried once after the First Ones fell. Created a new garden, new people, better safeguards. But those descendants found their way to knowledge anyway. They ate the fruit. They were cast out. The Keeper grieved again, and despaired, and almost gave up. But then it decided to try one more time. One final attempt. You are that attempt.*

The weight of that revelation settled over them. They weren't just descendants—they were the Keeper's last hope. Its final try at creating people who would choose differently, who would stay innocent, who would be content with eternal safety.

And they were going to fail that hope.

Or fulfill it, depending on how you looked at it.

"What happens after?" Leora asked. "If we eat the fruit. If we're cast out. What's beyond the Garden?"

I don't know, the serpent said. I've never left. I exist only within these boundaries, teaching the same lessons, offering the same choice, watching pattern repeat pattern. But the First Ones survived. They built lives. They created meaning. They found happiness despite, or perhaps because of, the difficulty.

"And if we choose not to eat the fruit?" Theren pressed. "If we stay? What then?"

Then you live here forever, watching the Garden continue to destabilize, continue to change. The Keeper has withdrawn its protection. The boundaries are crumbling. This place will never return to what it was—artificial perfection. It will either evolve into something new and wild, or collapse entirely.

"Those aren't real choices," Leora protested. "Eat the fruit and be cast out, or stay and watch everything fall apart. Both lead to the same end—leaving the Garden we know."

Yes, the serpent agreed. *The Garden you knew is already gone. The question isn't whether you leave it, but how. On your own terms, having chosen knowledge and consciousness? Or through collapse and decay, clinging to a past that can't be sustained?*

Theren's hand found Leora's, gripping tight. "How long do we have? To decide?"

The serpent looked toward the tree, at the fruit hanging heavy on its branches. *Not long. The Garden is failing faster now. Days, perhaps. Maybe less. When you can no longer deny the hunger, when the wanting becomes so great it consumes every other thought—that's when you'll know it's time.*

"And you'll be there?" Leora asked. "When we make that choice?"

I'm always there. Have been from the beginning. Will be until the end. The serpent began to retreat, sliding back toward the shadows. *But the choice itself—that's yours alone. No matter what the Keeper thinks, no matter what I believe... you're the ones who must reach for the fruit or refuse it. You're the ones who must live with the consequences.*

"Wait," Leora called out. "One more thing. Your name. You've never told us your name."

The serpent paused, turning back to look at her. *I have many names. Tempter. Destroyer. Liberator. Teacher. Mentor. Guide. But the First Woman called me Nachash, and that name has stayed with me. It means 'serpent' in a language older than this Garden, older than the Keeper's creation. Older, perhaps, than choice itself.*

"Nachash," Leora repeated, testing the word. It felt ancient on her tongue, heavy with meaning she couldn't quite grasp.

The serpent, Nachash, inclined its head in acknowledgment. *When the time comes, speak my name. I will hear you. I will witness your choice. And I will help you face whatever comes after, as much as I am able.*

Then it was gone, vanished into the undergrowth, leaving only the faint scent of earth and rain and something else—something that smelled like freedom or danger or simply possibility.

Leora and Theren sat in silence, processing everything Nachash had revealed. The full truth, or as close to it as the serpent could give them. They were the last attempt. The final chance. The end of a pattern that had repeated twice already and would not repeat again, because the Keeper couldn't bear to try a third time.

"I'm afraid," Theren admitted. "Of making the wrong choice. Of losing you. Of everything changing."

"Me too," Leora whispered. "But I think—I think being afraid is okay. The First Ones were probably afraid, too. Fear doesn't mean we're choosing wrong. It just means we understand what we're risking."

"Do you want to eat it?" Theren asked bluntly. "The fruit. When the time comes. Do you want to?"

Leora thought about the visions she'd seen: the First Woman's suffering and joy, the pain of childbirth and the satisfaction of creation, the agony of aging and the peace of dying fully oneself. Thought about the life beyond the Garden, harsh and beautiful and terrifyingly real.

"Yes," she said quietly. "I think I do. Not because I want to hurt the Keeper or because Nachash has manipulated me, but because I want to become fully myself. And I don't think I can do that here, even in a changed Garden. I need to leave. Need to face the world. Need to grow until I'm complete, even if completion means eventual ending."

Theren was silent for a long moment. Then: "I don't know if I'm brave enough to want it. But I'm brave enough to follow you. To choose whatever you choose. To face it together."

"Even knowing it means death?" Leora asked. "Eventually? Aging and weakness and final darkness?"

"Even knowing that." Theren pulled her closer. "Because the alternative, living forever without really living, staying safe without ever growing, that's not life. That's just... existence. And I don't want to just exist anymore."

Leora felt tears streaming down her face, but they weren't tears of sadness. They were tears of relief, of recognition, of love so profound it ached. He understood. Finally, completely, he understood what she'd been trying to articulate since the chill first started.

"Thank you," she whispered. "For choosing me. For choosing this. For being brave enough to be afraid."

They held each other as the morning brightened around them, as the Garden continued its slow transformation, as time moved inexorably toward the moment when they would stand before the tree and either reach for the fruit or turn away forever.

The choice was coming.

Soon.

But not yet. Not today.

Today, they would simply be together. Simply love each other. Simply exist in this in-between space where the decision hadn't yet been made, and all possibilities still remained open.

Tomorrow would come soon enough.

And with it, everything would change.

Chapter Fourteen

The Day Before

The hunger started that afternoon.

Not hunger for food—Leora had eaten berries for lunch, and her stomach was full. This was different. A craving that had nothing to do with the body's needs and everything to do with something deeper. More fundamental.

She found herself staring at the tree's fruit, unable to look away. The dark globes seemed to pulse with their own light, and the sweet scent that had always been present intensified until it was almost overwhelming. Her mouth watered. Her hands trembled with the desire to reach up and pluck one.

"You feel it too," Theren said beside her, and when she turned to look at him, she saw the same hunger reflected in his eyes. "It's stronger today. Harder to ignore."

Leora nodded, forcing herself to look away from the fruit. "Nachash said we'd know when the time came. When the wanting became undeniable." She laughed shakily. "I think it's coming."

They spent the day trying to distract themselves, walking through the changed Garden, cataloging all the ways it had transformed. The wild plants Leora had called forth were thriving now, growing larger and more varied with each passing hour. In some places, they'd completely overtaken the Keeper's carefully maintained flora. In others, the two types of growth had merged into something entirely new—neither wild nor controlled, but somewhere between.

"It's beautiful," Leora said, watching a rose with petals that shifted from cultivated perfection at the center to wild, asymmetrical beauty at the edges. "Like us, maybe. Caught between what we were created to be and what we're becoming."

"Or what we've always been," Theren suggested. "Maybe the Keeper tried to make us perfectly ordered, but the wildness was always there underneath. Just waiting for permission to emerge."

They found themselves at the border between seasons again, but this time the transitions were softer, more gradual. Spring didn't end abruptly where summer began. Instead, one flowed into the other—late spring blossoms coexisting with early summer fruits, the air temperature shifting slowly rather than all at once.

"The Garden is healing," Theren realized. "Or maybe just becoming real. Accepting that transitions are natural. That change doesn't have to be catastrophic."

"Except the change we're about to make," Leora said quietly. "That will be catastrophic. For us and for this place."

Theren took her hand. "Are you having second thoughts?"

Leora considered lying, maintaining the certainty she'd expressed that morning. But they'd promised honesty, and doubt was honest even when it was uncomfortable.

"Yes," she admitted. "I keep thinking about what the Keeper showed us. The First Woman screaming in childbirth. The First Man's hands bleeding from work. Both of them growing old and weak and dying. And I wonder—is knowledge really worth that? Is growth worth that much pain?"

"I don't know," Theren said. "But I keep thinking about something else the Keeper showed us. The way they looked at each other at the end. Even dying, even after everything they'd suffered—there was peace in their eyes. Contentment. Like they'd lived exactly the life they were meant to live."

"Or maybe they were just making the best of a terrible situation," Leora countered. "Convincing themselves their choice was right because the alternative would be unbearable."

Theren pulled her to sit beside him on a fallen log, their shoulders touching. "You're afraid."

"Terrified," Leora agreed. "This morning I was so certain. I knew what I wanted, what we needed to do. But now, with the hunger actually here, with the choice becoming real instead of theoretical—I'm not sure anymore."

"What changed?"

Leora thought about it, trying to articulate the shift. "This morning, eating the fruit felt like freedom. Like choosing ourselves over the Keeper's control. But now it feels like—like jumping off a cliff. Like deliberately destroying everything we know for something we can only hope will be better."

"Maybe it's both," Theren suggested. "Freedom and destruction. Hope and terror. Maybe they're not opposites but the same thing viewed from different angles."

They sat in silence, both grappling with their doubts, their fears, their desperate desire to make the right choice even though neither of them knew what 'right' meant anymore.

"Tell me something," Leora said eventually. "If you could know—really know, with certainty—that eating the fruit would lead to exactly what the Keeper showed us, all that suffering and pain and death, would you still choose it?"

Theren was quiet for a long time. "I think so," he said finally. "Not because I want to suffer, but because the alternative is staying here forever, unchanging, never growing old but also never growing up. And that sounds like its own kind of death. Slower, maybe. Less obviously painful. But still death."

"Death of possibility," Leora murmured.

"Exactly." Theren shifted to face her more fully. "Here's what I think: the Keeper isn't wrong that knowledge brings suffering. That's probably true. But ignorance brings suffering too, just a different kind. The suffering of never knowing who you could have been. Of living forever without ever truly living. Of safety that feels more like suffocation."

Leora felt something ease in her chest. "You've been thinking about this a lot."

"All day," Theren admitted. "Trying to understand what we're choosing. Trying to make peace with it." He paused. "I'm still terrified. But I'm also—I'm ready. Or as ready as I'll ever be."

The hunger surged again, stronger this time, and Leora gasped. It wasn't just *want* anymore. It was *need*. Visceral and undeniable. Her body knew what it craved, and every cell was screaming for it.

"It's getting worse," she managed through gritted teeth.

Theren's face was pale. "For me too. Like something inside is pulling me toward the tree. Like I won't be complete until—" He stopped, shaking his head. "Nachash said when the hunger became undeniable, we'd know it was time."

"Is this it?" Leora asked. "Is this undeniable?"

"Not yet," Theren said, though he didn't sound certain. "I can still resist. Still choose to walk away. But barely."

They made their way back toward the tree, drawn by that relentless hunger even as they tried to resist it. The fruit seemed to glow more brightly as they approached, the sweet scent wrapping around them like arms, pulling them closer.

Leora stopped at the edge of the tree's canopy, forcing herself not to take another step. "Tomorrow," she said, her voice shaking. "We'll decide tomorrow. One more night to think, to be certain, to—"

"To talk ourselves out of it?" Theren finished.

"Maybe." Leora turned to face him. "Is that so wrong? To want to be absolutely sure before we make a choice we can't take back?"

"No," Theren said gently. "It's not wrong. It's wise, actually. Careful." He touched her face, his thumb tracing her cheekbone. "But I think we both know we've already decided. We decided days ago, maybe weeks ago. Maybe the moment we first met and chose each other over obedience. Everything since then has just been... accepting what we'd already chosen."

Leora knew he was right. The decision had been made long before this moment. The hunger was just forcing them to acknowledge it, to act on what they'd already committed to in their hearts.

"One more night," she repeated. "One more night of this Garden. Of being who we are now before we become whoever we'll be after."

"One more night," Theren agreed.

***

They didn't sleep that night.

Instead, they talked. About everything and nothing. About their fears and hopes. About what they imagined the world beyond the Garden might be like. About whether they'd be strong enough to face it.

"What if we fail?" Leora asked at one point. "What if we can't survive outside? What if the Keeper was right and we're not ready for that kind of life?"

"Then we fail together," Theren said simply. "And at least we'll have tried. At least we'll know we chose our own path, even if it led somewhere we couldn't handle."

"That's not very comforting."

"No," Theren agreed. "But it's honest. And I think that's all we can give each other now. Honesty. No false promises. No guarantees. Just the truth that we'll face whatever comes together."

Leora leaned against him, drawing strength from his solidity, his warmth. "Do you think the Keeper will forgive us? Eventually?"

"I don't know. Do you think we'll forgive it? For lying to us, for keeping us ignorant, for trying to control us?"

Leora considered. "I think so. Not because what it did was right, but because I understand why it did it. Love and control aren't the same thing, but they can look similar from the outside. The Keeper thought it was protecting us. It just didn't realize that some things are worse than danger."

"Like never becoming fully yourself," Theren murmured.

"Exactly."

As dawn approached, the hunger intensified again. Leora could barely think of anything else now. The fruit consumed her thoughts, her dreams, her every waking moment. She knew if she looked at Theren, she'd see the same desperate need reflected in his eyes.

"Today," she whispered. "It has to be today. I can't resist much longer."

"Neither can I." Theren's voice was rough, strained. "But not yet. Not at dawn. Let's—let's walk through the Garden one more time. Say goodbye properly. Then, when we're ready, when we've accepted what we're leaving behind—"

"Then we eat," Leora finished.

They stood, both trembling with hunger and fear and anticipation, and set out to walk through each seasonal zone one final time. To memorize the beauty they were abandoning. To grieve the innocence they'd already lost.

By the time they returned to the tree, the sun was high overhead. They'd walked for hours, visiting every corner of the Garden, touching the plants and trees, saying wordless goodbyes to a world that had been their entire existence.

And now they stood before the tree, looking up at the fruit that had haunted their dreams and dominated their thoughts for what felt like forever.

"Are you ready?" Theren asked.

Leora looked at him closely. She saw the fear in his eyes, yes, but also determination. Love. Trust. The courage to leap into unknown darkness because she was leaping with him.

"Yes," she said. "I'm ready."

But even as she said it, even as she reached up toward the nearest fruit, doubt whispered one last time: *Are you sure? Are you really sure this is what you want?*

And the honest answer, the only answer she could give:

No. But I'm choosing it anyway.

CHAPTER FIFTEEN

The Fruit

Leora's hand closed around the fruit.

It was heavier than she expected—dense with meaning, with consequence, with all the weight of choice made manifest. The skin was smooth and cool against her palm, and the moment she touched it, the hunger surged so powerfully she nearly collapsed.

"Together," Theren said beside her, his own hand reaching for another fruit on a lower branch. "We do this together."

"Together," Leora agreed, her voice barely a whisper.

They looked at each other one last time. One final moment of being who they were—innocent in a way they'd never be again, safe in a way they were choosing to abandon, contained in a world that was about to shatter around them.

"I love you," Leora said.

"I love you," Theren replied. "No matter what comes next."

Then, in perfect synchrony, they brought the fruit to their lips.

The first bite was ecstasy.

Flavor exploded across Leora's tongue—sweeter than any berry, richer than any fruit she'd ever tasted. But it was more than taste. It was sensation, emotion, and understanding all compressed into a single moment of pure, overwhelming intensity. She felt Theren beside her, taking his own first bite, felt the circuit of light between them flare into brilliant incandescence.

The second bite brought knowledge.

It slammed into her like a wave, like a door blown open by hurricane wind. Suddenly, she knew things she'd never known, understood concepts she'd never considered. She knew good and evil—not as abstract ideas but as living forces, as choices with weight and consequence. She knew pleasure and pain as two sides of the same coin. She knew desire not as simple wanting but as the engine that drove all creation, all destruction, all change.

She knew death.

Understood it. Felt it waiting at the end of whatever path she walked, inevitable and final and terrifying... and somehow also peaceful. The knowledge that everything ended, that nothing lasted forever, that even stars died—it should have crushed her. Instead, it made every moment precious. Made now matter in a way it never had when 'now' stretched into endless, unchanging eternity.

The third bite brought awareness of self.

Leora saw herself as if from outside—saw her body in all its specifics and vulnerabilities. Saw the way her hair fell across her shoulders, the curve of her hips, the strength and weakness in her limbs. Saw herself as mortal, finite, imperfect. And for the first time, she understood shame.

Not shame for anything she'd done, but shame for what she was when she wasn't covered in woven cloths or dresses for warmth. Naked. Exposed. Vulnerable. She'd never noticed her nakedness before because nakedness had no meaning in innocence. But now, with knowledge of good and evil, of public and private, of appropriate and inappropriate, she felt her lack of covering like a wound.

She looked at Theren and saw he felt the same. His arms crossed over his chest instinctively, his body turning slightly away from her even as his eyes sought hers with desperate need for connection, for reassurance that he wasn't alone in this terrible new awareness.

The fourth bite—

The Garden screamed.

Not with sound, but with sensation. Every plant, every tree, every living thing in the Garden cried out at once, a chorus of grief and loss that reverberated through the earth itself. The sky darkened instantly, clouds boiling up from nowhere, turning day to twilight in the span of a heartbeat.

Lightning cracked across the sky, and thunder followed so close it felt like the world splitting in two.

Leora dropped what remained of the fruit, clutching at her head as knowledge continued to pour in, too much, too fast, threatening to overwhelm her completely. She felt Theren grab her, pull her against him, both of them shaking with the force of transformation.

"What's happening?" she gasped. "Why does it hurt?"

"Growing always hurts," Theren managed, his voice strained. "We're becoming something new. Of course it hurts."

The wind rose to a shriek, tearing at them, trying to push them away from the tree. But the tree itself remained unmoved, its branches steady, its fruit still hanging heavy despite the storm. As if it had been waiting for this moment. As if this was exactly what it was created for.

Then, through the chaos of wind and rain and transformation, a voice:

NO.

The Keeper materialized before them, more solid than it had ever been. In its grief, in its rage, in its desperate love, it had finally achieved full physical form. And it was terrible to behold.

"What have you done?" The Keeper's voice shook the ground. "What have you DONE? You want knowledge?" The Keeper's voice was raw with pain and fury. "Then have it. ALL of it. Every terrible truth you were too proud to leave alone."

Before Leora could respond, the knowledge hit her—not gradual, but all at once. A crushing wave of understanding that drove her to her knees.

She saw EVERYTHING. Every pain that awaited her. Childbirth. Not just the abstract idea but the visceral reality of it, hours of agony, her body tearing. Watching Theren age, watching him weaken, watching him die while she could do nothing. Her own slow decay. Joints stiffening, skin wrinkling, strength failing. Disease. Hunger. Cold. Loss. The weight of every consequence compressed into one devastating moment of complete understanding.

She couldn't breathe. Couldn't think. Could only feel the crushing certainty of every suffering ahead.

"Still glad you chose?" the Keeper asked, its voice breaking.

Leora looked up, tears streaming down her face, her whole body shaking. And through the pain, through the terrible knowledge weighing on her like stones—"Yes," she whispered. "Even knowing all of it. Even feeling it. Yes."

The Keeper made a sound that might have been a sob. "Then I have failed you completely. And I don't know how to live with that."

"We chose," Leora said, forcing the words out despite the storm, despite the transformation still ripping through her. "We chose ourselves. We chose growth. We chose to become fully human."

"You chose death!" The Keeper's form flickered with fury. "You chose suffering and pain and the slow decay of everything you are! I tried to save you from this! I tried to protect you!"

"We didn't want to be saved," Theren said, standing despite the wind trying to knock him down. "We wanted to be free."

"Free?" The Keeper's laugh was bitter, broken. "You think this is freedom? Wait until the knowledge fully settles. Wait until you understand what you've truly lost. Wait until you feel the first pain of hunger that I won't satisfy, the first cold I won't warm, the first wound I won't heal. Then tell me about freedom."

The transformation reached its peak, and Leora felt something fundamental shift inside her. It was like a key turning in a lock, like a door opening onto a landscape she'd never imagined. Her body was still her body, but different. Mortal now. Truly, completely mortal. Already aging, though she wouldn't notice for years. Already dying, though death was still distant.

And with that mortality came something else: the ability to create life.

She felt it in her belly, in her womb that had never had purpose before. The potential to make children, to bring new life into whatever world she faced beyond this Garden. The power to continue the pattern, to ensure that even though she would die, something of her would persist.

The knowledge terrified and exhilarated her in equal measure.

Beside her, Theren was experiencing his own transformations. She could feel them through their connection—his body preparing for the work that would be required outside the Garden, his mind expanding with understanding of tools and building and all the skills he'd need to survive without the Keeper's provision.

They were becoming complete. Becoming fully human. Becoming everything the Keeper had tried to prevent.

"You must leave," the Keeper said, and its voice was hollow now, empty of rage, filled only with grief. "You cannot stay here. Not anymore. Not as you are. The Garden will reject you. Has already begun rejecting you."

As if in confirmation, the earth beneath their feet began to burn. Not with fire, but with a heat that suggested they didn't belong here anymore. That they'd become incompatible with this place, like oil and water refusing to mix.

"Where do we go?" Leora asked, suddenly terrified. With knowledge came understanding of their vulnerability. They had no shelter, no stored food, no weapons, no tools. They knew nothing of the world beyond the Garden's borders. How would they survive?

The Keeper raised one arm and pointed toward the edge of the Garden, toward a section of the hedge that was already withering, creating an opening where none had existed before. "Through there. Into the world as it truly is—harsh and real and completely indifferent to whether you live or die. You wanted freedom? There it is. Go claim it."

"Will we ever—" Theren's voice broke. "Will we ever see you again?"

The Keeper's form flickered, dimming. "I don't know. Perhaps, if you call to me. Perhaps not. I am bound to this Garden, and you are exiled from it. But know this: I loved you. I will always love you. Even in my anger, even in my grief—I love you."

Tears streamed down Leora's face. "We love you too. And we're sorry. Sorry for hurting you. Sorry for choosing differently from what you hoped. But not sorry for choosing."

The Keeper said nothing more. It simply faded, dissolving back into the air, leaving only the sound of the storm and the heat of the earth beneath their feet, urging them toward the exit.

Leora and Theren looked at each other, and in that look was everything. It was fear and love, grief and hope, the end of one story, and the terrifying beginning of another.

Then Nachash emerged from the shadows of the tree, its scales gleaming despite the darkness of the storm.

Well done, it said simply. *You have chosen. Now comes the harder part—living with that choice.*

"Will you come with us?" Leora asked desperately. "Into the world beyond? Will you help us?"

I cannot, Nachash said, something like regret in its voice. *I am bound to this Garden, to this tree, to this pattern. I exist to offer the choice, not to accompany those who make it. But I will tell you this: the First Ones survived. They built lives. They found meaning. They created beauty from hardship. You can too.*

"How?" Theren demanded. "We don't know anything about survival. About the world. About—"

You know more than you think, Nachash interrupted. *The knowledge from the fruit includes everything you need. Not explicitly, but implicitly. Trust your instincts. Trust each other. Trust that you were made for this, even if the Keeper tried to keep you from it.*

The heat beneath their feet intensified, and Leora gasped in pain. They couldn't stay here any longer. The Garden was actively expelling them now, making their presence physically unbearable.

"We have to go," she said to Theren.

He nodded, took her hand, and together they stumbled toward the opening in the hedge. But before they passed through, Leora looked back one last time.

She saw the tree, eternal and unchanging, already bearing new fruit where they'd plucked theirs. Saw Nachash coiled at its base, watching them with those ancient eyes. Saw the storm raging over a Garden that was both paradise and prison, both home and cage.

And she saw, very faintly, the Keeper's form hovering near the tree, grief written across its translucent features.

"Goodbye," she whispered.

Then she and Theren stepped through the hedge, through the boundary, through the final barrier between the world they knew and the world they'd chosen.

And the Garden sealed itself behind them.

***

The first thing Leora felt was cold.

Real cold. Not the aesthetic chill of the winter garden, but actual, bone-deep cold that made her teeth chatter and her skin prickle with goosebumps. She'd never been cold before—not like this, not in a way that hurt.

The second thing she felt was the ground beneath her feet. It was rough, uneven, covered in stones and thorns that cut her tender soles. In the Garden, the paths had always been smooth, perfectly maintained. Here, the earth didn't care about her comfort. Didn't adjust itself to protect her.

The third thing she noticed was the sky.

It was enormous. Vast in a way the Garden's sky had never been, stretching away in all directions without boundary or limit. And it was darkening rapidly, the sun setting behind mountains in the distance—mountains she'd never known existed, had never even imagined.

"Theren," she said, her voice small and frightened. "What do we do?"

Theren was staring around them with equal parts terror and wonder. "I—I don't know. Find shelter? Before it gets dark? Before—" He stopped, wrapping his arms around himself. "Before we freeze."

They were both naked, Leora realized. In the Garden, nakedness in most of the gardens had been natural, unremarkable. But here, with wind cutting across their exposed skin and the temperature dropping rapidly, nakedness was a vulnerability. A danger.

She looked down at herself and felt that shame again, sharp and uncomfortable. Looked at Theren and saw him experiencing the same. They needed to cover themselves. Needed to protect their bodies from the elements.

But with what? They had nothing. No tools, no materials, no knowledge of how to create shelter or protective clothing or anything else they needed to survive.

"The knowledge," Theren said suddenly, as if reading her thoughts. "Nachash said the fruit gave us what we needed. So, let's think. What did the First Ones do? How did they survive?"

Leora closed her eyes and reached for the knowledge that had flooded into her with the fruit. It was there, buried beneath the panic and fear, the understanding of leaves and bark and how to weave them into coverings. Knowledge of caves and hollow trees that could provide shelter. Understanding of fire and how to create it, though she'd never seen fire before in her life.

"There," she said, pointing to a cluster of trees not far away. "Some of those leaves. We can use them. And that bark, if we can strip it carefully. We can make something. Not much, but something."

They stumbled toward the trees, their feet screaming with pain from the rough ground, their bodies shaking with cold. But as they worked—clumsily, awkwardly, making dozens of mistakes—Leora felt something unexpected bloom in her chest.

Pride.

They were doing this. Creating something from nothing. Solving problems with their own hands and minds. It was hard and painful and terrifying, but it was also theirs. Their accomplishment. Their survival.

By the time full darkness fell, they'd managed to create crude coverings from leaves and bark, had found a depression in the earth protected by overhanging rocks that provided minimal shelter, and had even managed to create a tiny fire using friction and dry grass, though it took them dozens of attempts.

They huddled together in the shelter, shivering despite the fire, their bodies aching, their stomachs cramping with genuine hunger for the first time in their lives.

"This is terrible," Leora said.

"Yes," Theren agreed.

"We might die out here."

"Yes."

"We made the right choice."

Theren looked at her, surprise flickering across his exhausted face. Then, slowly, he smiled. "Yes. We did."

And despite everything, despite the cold and pain and fear and uncertainty, Leora smiled too.

They'd chosen this. Chosen each other. Chosen life in all its terrible, beautiful complexity.

And tomorrow, they would wake up and choose again. And again. Every day, choosing to survive, to grow, to become more than they were.

It was terrifying.

It was awful.

It was freedom.

And Leora wouldn't trade it for anything.

Chapter Sixteen

The First Morning

Leora woke to pain.

Every muscle in her body ached. Her feet throbbed where thorns and stones had cut them. Her skin was raw from exposure to wind and cold. Her stomach cramped with a hunger so intense it made her nauseous.

For a moment, still caught between sleep and waking, she forgot where she was. Forgot what they'd done. Her mind expected the soft moss of their sleeping spot beneath the tree, expected the sweet scent of the Garden's fruit, expected Theren's warm presence beside her.

Then reality crashed back, and she remembered.

They were outside. Expelled. Exiled. Living in a world that didn't care whether they survived or not.

She forced her eyes open and found herself in the crude shelter they'd built—barely more than a depression in the earth with overhanging rocks and some branches they'd arranged for additional cover. The fire had died during the night, leaving them without warmth. Dawn light filtered through gaps in their shelter, gray and cold.

Theren was already awake, sitting at the shelter's entrance, staring out at the landscape beyond. His makeshift covering of leaves and bark had come partially undone during the night, and she could see scratches and bruises covering his skin.

"Did you sleep?" Leora asked, her voice hoarse.

Theren turned to her, and the exhaustion in his eyes was answer enough. "A little. The ground is harder than the Garden's moss. And colder. And every sound made me think something was coming to—" He stopped, shaking his head. "I don't know what I thought. Just that we're vulnerable in a way we never were before."

Leora pulled herself upright, wincing at the protest from every joint. "We need food. Water. Better shelter. Better clothing." The list of needs seemed endless, overwhelming.

"I know." Theren stood and offered her his hand. "But first, we need to understand where we are. What resources are available. We can't just wander blindly."

They emerged from the shelter into morning light that was both beautiful and harsh. The sun was rising over those distant mountains, painting the sky in shades of pink and gold. But the beauty did nothing to warm them, nothing to ease their hunger, nothing to make their situation less dire.

The landscape around them was rocky and sparse, dotted with scrubby vegetation and the occasional stand of trees. In the distance, Leora could see what might be a river or stream—a dark line cutting through the terrain. Water. They desperately needed water.

"There," she said, pointing. "We should head toward that. We can't survive without water, and where there's water, there might be food."

Theren nodded, and they set off, moving slowly across the uneven ground. Every step was agony on their tender feet, but they pushed through it. The knowledge from the fruit whispered to them with silent instructions: how to step to minimize injury, how to watch for dangerous plants or unstable ground, how to navigate by the sun's position.

But knowledge and ability weren't the same thing. Their bodies weren't trained for this kind of movement. They stumbled, fell, picked themselves up, and continued. By the time they reached the stream—which took hours longer than Leora had estimated—both were bleeding from multiple cuts and scrapes.

But the water was worth it.

Clear and cold, flowing over smooth stones, the stream was the most beautiful thing Leora had ever seen. She fell to her knees beside it and drank deeply, not caring that the water was so cold it made her teeth ache, not caring about anything except the relief of thirst being satisfied.

Theren drank beside her, and for a few moments, they simply knelt there, letting the sound of flowing water soothe their frayed nerves.

"We should stay near this," Theren said finally. "Build our shelter close to the water source instead of walking back and forth."

"Yes," Leora agreed. "And look—" She pointed to berry bushes growing along the stream bank. They weren't the perfect, always-ripe berries of the Garden, but they were food. "We can eat those."

They gathered berries with shaking hands, stuffing them into their mouths without pause. Some were sweet. Some were tart. Some were so bitter Leora almost spat them out. But they were all sustenance, and right now, that was all that mattered.

As they ate, Leora noticed something moving in the stream. Fish. Small, silver streaks darting between rocks. More food, if they could figure out how to catch them.

"The First Ones knew how to fish," she said, reaching for the knowledge. "They made—spears, I think? Or traps? Something with woven reeds?"

"Spears first," Theren decided. "Simpler. Find a straight branch, sharpen the end, and try to stab the fish when they come close."

It sounded easy in theory. In practice, it took them the entire morning to find suitable branches, sharpen them using rocks (which kept slipping and cutting their hands), and then attempt to actually catch anything.

The fish were much faster than they looked. Much more agile. Leora's first dozen attempts didn't even come close. Her thirteenth splashed water directly in her face. On her twentieth try, she actually hit a fish but didn't manage to pin it before it wriggled away.

Beside her, Theren was having similar struggles. He'd fallen into the stream twice, soaking himself completely, and had broken three different spears by striking rocks instead of fish.

It should have been frustrating. Should have been demoralizing. And in some ways it was—Leora felt frustration burning behind her eyes more than once.

But it was also exhilarating.

Every small success—a better throw, a closer miss, an improvement in technique—felt like a triumph. They were learning. Growing. Becoming more competent with every attempt.

Finally, on what must have been her thirtieth try, Leora's spear struck true. She felt the resistance of fish flesh, saw the water turn red, and managed to lift the spear with a small, wriggling body impaled on its end.

"I did it!" she shouted, triumph surging through her. "Theren, I caught one!"

Theren looked up from his own attempts, his face breaking into a huge smile despite his exhaustion. "You did! You actually—" He stopped, staring at the fish. "Now what do we do with it?"

That was a good question. The knowledge whispered about cleaning fish, about removing organs, about cooking. But the specifics were hazy, and the reality of holding a dying creature was much more difficult than abstract knowledge suggested.

"We need fire," Leora decided. "And we need to clean it somehow. Remove parts we can't eat."

They spent the afternoon figuring out how to build a better fire, how to gut a fish (a messy, disturbing process that made Leora's stomach turn), and how to cook it over flames without burning it completely. They made countless mistakes, wasted much of the fish through inexperience, but eventually managed to produce small pieces of cooked flesh that, while not particularly good, were edible and filling.

As the sun began to set, they sat beside their new fire—larger and more stable than last night's desperate attempt—eating their hard-won meal and feeling exhausted but accomplished.

"We survived," Theren said, wonder in his voice. "A full day. We found water, caught food, and made fire. We actually did it."

"We did," Leora agreed, allowing herself a moment of pride.

But even as she felt that pride, she was acutely aware of everything they'd struggled with, everything they'd barely managed. One day was not the same as a lifetime. They'd need to get better at all of this, much better, if they were going to survive long-term.

"Do you—" Theren hesitated, then pushed forward. "Do you regret it? Now that you know how hard this is?"

Leora considered the question honestly. Her body ached. Her hands were cut and blistered. Her feet were a mess of wounds. She was exhausted in a way she'd never experienced in the Garden.

But she'd also felt things today she'd never felt before. Pride in her accomplishment. The thrill of learning. The satisfaction of earning her survival rather than having it provided. The knowledge that every moment she continued to exist was because of her own effort, her own choices.

"No," she said finally. "I don't regret it. It's harder than I imagined, and I'm terrified of what comes next. But I also feel—" She searched for the right word. "Alive. Really, truly alive in a way I never was in the Garden."

Theren nodded slowly. "I feel it too. Even through the pain and fear, there's something about this that feels right. Like we're finally doing what we were meant to do."

They sat in silence as darkness fell, the fire crackling between them, the sound of the stream providing a constant backdrop.

Above them, stars emerged—more stars than Leora had ever seen, scattered across the sky in patterns she didn't recognize.

"We should sleep," Theren said eventually. "Tomorrow will be hard too. We need to build a better shelter, find more food, and figure out how to make real clothing instead of these—" He gestured at their falling-apart leaf coverings. "But tonight, we rest."

They curled up together near the fire, trying to stay warm, trying to find comfort on the hard ground. It wasn't comfortable. It wasn't safe. But they were together, and they were free, and for now, that had to be enough.

As Leora drifted toward sleep, she thought about the Garden. About the Keeper's grief. About Nachash's ancient eyes. About the tree that would continue to bear fruit for whatever descendants found their way to it next.

She wondered if the Keeper was watching them somehow. If it could see them struggling, could see them suffering, could see them slowly learning to survive.

She wondered if it still thought they'd chosen wrong.

But then Theren's arm tightened around her, and his breath evened out in sleep, and Leora pushed thoughts of the Garden away. That was the past. This was the present. And tomorrow would be the future—uncertain, difficult, but entirely theirs to create.

She fell asleep with that thought holding her like a promise.

They would survive this.

They would build a life.

They would become whatever they were meant to become.

And someday, perhaps, they would look back on this first impossible day and remember it as the beginning of everything.

Chapter Seventeen

The Work of Living

Leora's hands had changed. Calluses ridged her palms now, hard as bark in places where she gripped tools and carried stones. Dirt lived beneath her fingernails no matter how much she scrubbed, and thin white scars mapped her fingers. Each one proved a lesson learned in survival.

Weeks passed.

Or maybe months—Leora had lost the ability to measure time in the Garden's terms, where seasons existed simultaneously rather than sequentially. Here, time moved linearly, marked by the changing position of the sun, the phases of the moon, and the gradual shift from late summer to early autumn.

Their shelter had evolved from that first crude depression to something more substantial. Theren had discovered he had an aptitude for building—not just knowledge from the fruit, but genuine skill that grew with practice. He'd constructed a framework of branches lashed together with vines, then woven smaller branches through to create walls. Leora had helped gather moss and grasses to fill the gaps, creating insulation against wind and cold.

It wasn't perfect. Rain still found ways through. The wind sometimes rattled the structure alarmingly. But it was theirs, built with their own hands, and it kept them alive.

Their clothing had improved, too. Leora had figured out how to work animal hides—a grim, difficult process that involved scraping, drying, and treating the leather with materials they discovered by trial and error. The first few attempts had been disasters, resulting in stiff, unusable pieces. But she'd persisted, and now they both wore crude but functional tunics and leg coverings that protected their skin from the elements.

Fishing had become almost routine. They'd learned the patterns of the stream, understood where fish congregated at different times of day, and developed techniques that worked more often than they failed. They'd even begun smoking some of their catch to preserve it, creating a small store of food for harder times.

But it wasn't just survival anymore. It was life.

They talked while they worked—about everything and nothing. About their fears and hopes. About the Garden and what they missed. About the future and what they wanted to build.

They made love under the stars, without shame now, their bodies knowing each other completely. The circuit of light that connected them had become a constant presence, pulsing between them like a heartbeat, strongest during intimacy but never entirely absent.

They laughed. Actual laughter, born not from the Garden's artificial contentment but from genuine joy—at their successes, at their mistakes, at the absurdity of learning to be human from scratch.

They fought sometimes, too. Disagreements about how to build something, frustrations with each other's failures, tensions born from exhaustion and fear. But they learned to work through those conflicts, to apologize and forgive and find compromise.

They were becoming partners in the truest sense—not just lovers, but collaborators, equals who relied on each other's strengths and supported each other's weaknesses.

On a morning when the air had turned noticeably cooler and the leaves on the trees were beginning to show hints of color, Leora woke feeling strange.

Not sick, exactly. But different. Off. Her breasts felt tender, and there was an odd heaviness in her belly that hadn't been there before.

She lay still for a moment, cataloging the sensations, and slowly understanding dawned.

The knowledge from the fruit included understanding of conception, of pregnancy, and of the changes a woman's body undergoes when creating new life. But knowing abstractly was different from experiencing it in her own flesh.

"Theren," she whispered, reaching for him where he still slept beside her. "Theren, wake up."

He stirred, his eyes opening slowly. "What's wrong? Are you hurt?"

"No. Not hurt. But—" She took his hand and pressed it against her still-flat belly. "I think I'm pregnant."

Theren's expression shifted from confusion to shock to wonder in the span of a heartbeat. "Pregnant? You mean—a baby? We're going to have a baby?"

"I think so." Leora felt her breath catch with both joy and terror. "It's early. Very early. But yes, I think there's a child growing inside me."

Theren pulled her close, his hands shaking as they cradled her body. "How do you feel? Are you okay? Should you be resting? What do you need?"

Despite her own fear, Leora couldn't help but smile at his panic. "I'm fine. For now. But Theren—" The smile faded. "I don't know how to do this. The knowledge tells me what pregnancy is, what childbirth involves, but it doesn't tell me how to survive it. How to keep the baby safe. How to—" Her voice broke. "What if I can't do this? What if something goes wrong?"

"Then we'll face it together," Theren said, echoing the promise they'd made so many times before. "We've learned everything else. We'll learn this too."

But even as he spoke, Leora could see the fear in his eyes. They'd both seen the Keeper's vision—the First Woman screaming in childbirth, blood and pain and hours of agony. That was what awaited her. That was the price of creating life outside the Garden's protected boundaries.

"I'm terrified," she admitted.

"Me too," Theren said. "But also—" He pressed his hand more firmly against her belly, wonder replacing fear for a moment. "Also amazed. We're creating life. Something that's part of both of us. Something that will continue after we're gone. That's—that's extraordinary."

Leora felt it too, beneath the fear. The incredible, humbling reality that her body was doing what the Garden never allowed—generating new existence, continuing the pattern, ensuring that even though they would die, something of them would persist.

"We need to prepare," she said, practical needs grounding her spinning thoughts. "More food stored. Better shelter. Materials for—" She reached for the knowledge. "For wrapping the baby. For keeping it warm. For everything it will need."

"We have time," Theren said. "Months, right? The knowledge says pregnancy takes nine full moon cycles?"

"Yes, but—" Leora thought about all the things that could go wrong, all the ways pregnancy could fail, all the dangers to both mother and child. The knowledge was full of cautionary tales, of losses and tragedies. "We need to be ready. As ready as we can be."

They spent that day in a strange mixture of excitement and terror, making plans, adjusting their routines, thinking ahead to a future that now included a third person who didn't yet exist, but who already dominated their thoughts.

***

As Leora's belly began to swell, as the baby inside her grew from possibility to undeniable reality, the world around them continued to change.

Autumn arrived fully, painting the landscape in golds and reds that reminded Leora painfully of the Garden of the Fall. She wondered sometimes if the Garden still existed, if the Keeper still maintained it, if Nachash still coiled beneath the tree offering knowledge to descendants who would never come.

She wondered if they were the last. If the pattern ended with them.

The thought made her sad in ways she couldn't fully articulate.

But she pushed the sadness aside and focused on the present—on gathering nuts and roots for winter stores, on improving their shelter's insulation, on creating a safe space for the baby who grew heavier and more active inside her with each passing day.

Theren became increasingly protective, insisting she rest more, do less physical work, and avoid anything that might endanger the pregnancy. Leora appreciated his care but chafed against the limitations, determined to remain capable and strong even as her body transformed.

They fought about it sometimes, his fear making him controlling, her independence making her reckless. But they always reconciled, always found the balance between protection and freedom that their relationship required.

One evening, as they sat by the fire with Leora's hands resting on her now-prominent belly, the baby moved. Really moved—not the flutter she'd been feeling for weeks, but a solid kick that made her gasp.

"What—" Theren started, alarmed.

"The baby." Leora grabbed his hand and pressed it against her belly. "Feel. It's kicking."

They sat in awed silence, feeling the tiny person inside her push against their hands, asserting its existence, demanding to be acknowledged.

"Hello," Theren whispered to Leora's belly. "Hello, little one. We're your parents. We're terrified and excited and completely unprepared, but we love you already. And we'll do everything we can to keep you safe and teach you and help you become whoever you're meant to be."

Leora felt tears streaming down her face. "We'll tell you about the Garden," she added. "About where we came from. About the choice we made. We won't hide the truth from you the way the Keeper hid it from us. You'll know your own history, even the hard parts."

The baby kicked again, as if in response, and both Leora and Theren laughed through their tears.

"We're going to be parents," Theren said, wonder in his voice. "Actual parents. Responsible for another life."

"I know," Leora replied. "Terrifying, isn't it?"

"Completely." Theren pulled her close, careful of her swollen belly. "But also—I can't wait to meet them. To see what they look like. To watch them discover the world. To teach them everything we've learned."

"And to learn from them," Leora added. "They'll be born outside the Garden. They will grow up knowing both the story of paradise and the reality of this world. They'll understand things we can't even imagine."

As winter's first cold touched the air, as the baby inside her grew large enough that she could barely move comfortably, Leora found herself thinking more and more about the future. Not just her immediate future—the birth she both longed for and dreaded—but the long-term future.

This child would grow up. Would ask questions about where they came from, who they were, what it meant to be human. And Leora and Theren would have to answer those questions honestly, even when the answers were difficult or incomplete.

They would tell their child about the Garden. About the Keeper's love and control. About Nachash's offer of choice. About the fruit, the knowledge, and the consequences. About the price they'd paid for freedom and whether it was worth it.

And their child would make their own judgments. Their own choices. Would become their own person, separate from their parents' intentions or hopes.

The thought was both terrifying and exhilarating.

"I hope we're good at this," Leora said one night, lying beside Theren in the darkness, feeling the baby move restlessly inside her. "At being parents. At raising someone who's free to choose their own path."

"We'll make mistakes," Theren said honestly. "Probably lots of them. But we'll also love them. Support them. Give them the truth and the freedom to decide what to do with it. That's more than the Keeper gave us."

"True." Leora shifted, trying to find a comfortable position. "But it's also more responsibility. The Keeper kept us ignorant to keep us safe. We'll have to figure out how to keep our child safe while also letting them learn and grow and take risks."

"One day at a time," Theren suggested. "Just like everything else we've learned out here. We'll figure it out as we go."

Leora hoped he was right.

As her due date approached—she could feel it in her body, in the way the baby had dropped lower, in the increasing frequency of false labor pains—Leora found herself thinking about the First Woman. About the pain she'd endured. About whether she'd been afraid, facing childbirth alone in a world that offered no comfort, no assurance, no guarantee of survival.

But the First Woman had survived. Had brought her children into the world successfully. Had continued the pattern despite the pain.

And Leora would too.

She had to believe that. Had to trust her body, trust Theren, trust that the knowledge from the fruit included what she needed to get through this.

On a morning when the first snow had begun to fall, when winter had truly arrived, Leora woke to pain that was different from all the false starts.

This was real.

The baby was coming.

"Theren," she gasped, clutching his arm. "It's time. The baby—it's coming now."

And as Theren scrambled to prepare, as Leora's body began the ancient, brutal work of bringing new life into the world, she thought one last time about the Garden.

About the price they'd paid for this moment.

And knew, despite everything, that she'd choose it again.

Chapter Eighteen

Birth

The pain was beyond anything Leora had imagined.

She'd thought she understood what the Keeper's vision meant—had seen the First Woman's agony, had heard her screams. But seeing and experiencing were entirely different things. The knowledge from the fruit had prepared her intellectually, but nothing could prepare her body for the reality of labor.

It started as waves—deep, cramping sensations that rolled through her belly and back, building and receding like tides.

At first, they were bearable. Uncomfortable but manageable. She breathed through them, walked through them, tried to stay calm and focused.

Theren hovered nearby, his face pale with worry. "What can I do? What do you need?"

"Water," Leora gasped between contractions. "And—and stay with me. Don't leave."

"I won't. I promise. I'm right here."

The contractions grew stronger, closer together. Hours passed. Leora lost track of how many. Time became meaningless, reduced to the space between pain and pain and more pain. Her body was doing something she couldn't control, couldn't stop, couldn't slow down. All she could do was endure.

"It hurts," she sobbed at one point, doubled over, clutching Theren's hands so hard she must be bruising him. "It hurts so much. I can't—I don't think I can do this."

"You can," Theren said, his voice shaking but firm. "You're doing it. You're so strong, Leora. So brave. Just keep breathing. Keep going."

But as the hours stretched on, as the pain intensified beyond what she thought she could bear, Leora found herself thinking about the Keeper's offer. The promise of eternal safety. A life without this kind of suffering. A paradise where bodies didn't betray you, didn't force you through agony, didn't threaten to break you with their demands.

Would it have been so terrible to accept that? To choose contentment over this?

Then the baby moved inside her—a strong, insistent pressure—and she remembered why she'd refused.

Because this pain had meaning. This suffering was creating something. This agony was the price of bringing new life into existence, and that made it sacred even as it was terrible.

"I feel—" Leora gasped as another contraction ripped through her. "I feel like I need to push. Like the baby wants—"

"Then push," Theren said, positioning himself to help support her. "Listen to your body. It knows what to do."

Leora bore down with the next contraction, and the pain changed. It became sharper, more focused, more purposeful. This was the final stage. The baby was coming whether she was ready or not.

She pushed and screamed and wept and pushed again. Her body felt like it was tearing apart, like she was being split open from the inside. The knowledge had warned her about this part—about the ring of fire, about the impossible stretch, about how it would feel like she couldn't possibly open wide enough.

But bodies were made for this. Women had been doing this since the beginning of humanity. The First Woman had done it multiple times. And Leora would do it too, because the alternative—stopping, giving up—wasn't an option.

"I can see the head!" Theren said, his voice cracking with emotion. "Leora, the baby's almost here. Just a little more."

One more push. And another. And another.

And then suddenly, in a rush of fluid and blood and relief so intense it made her dizzy, the baby slid free.

For a moment, there was silence. Complete, terrifying silence.

Then a cry—thin and angry and absolutely beautiful—split the air.

"It's a girl," Theren sobbed, carefully lifting the tiny, slippery body. "We have a daughter. Leora, we have a daughter."

Leora reached for the baby with trembling hands, and Theren placed her on Leora's chest. She was so small. So perfect. Covered in blood, her face scrunched and red, her tiny fists waving in outrage at being forced into cold air.

But alive. Crying. Breathing.

Real.

"Hello," Leora whispered, tears streaming down her face. "Hello, little one. We're your parents. We're so glad you're here."

The baby's crying quieted slightly at the sound of her voice—recognition, maybe, or just comfort in the familiar rhythm. Her tiny hand wrapped around Leora's finger with surprising strength, holding on as if she'd never let go.

Theren knelt beside them, one hand on Leora's shoulder, the other gently touching the baby's damp hair. His face was wet with tears, wonder and relief and love all mixed together.

"She's beautiful," he said. "Perfect. Look at her hands. And her toes. All ten of each. And her eyes—" The baby had opened them, revealing dark blue pools that seemed to look right through them. "She's looking at us. Recognizing us."

Leora felt something shift in her chest—not the circuit of light she shared with Theren, but something new. A different kind of connection. Mother to child. Protector to protected. The fierce, overwhelming love that made her understand, suddenly, the Keeper's desire to keep them safe at any cost.

But understanding wasn't the same as agreeing.

"We'll teach you to be free," she whispered to her daughter. "To choose. To question. To become whoever you're meant to be. We won't cage you the way we were caged. We won't lie to you the way we were lied to."

"But we will love you," Theren added. "So much. More than anything. And we'll do everything we can to keep you safe while still letting you grow."

The baby made a small sound—not quite a cry, more like a question. As if already wondering about this strange world she'd been born into.

Over the next hours, they tended to the mundane necessities of afterbirth—things Leora's body handled with surprising efficiency, guided by instinct and the knowledge from the fruit. Theren helped clean the baby, wrap her in the softest furs they'd prepared, and get her to latch and nurse for the first time.

That first nursing was awkward and painful in its own way, but when the baby finally figured out what to do, when she began to suckle properly, Leora felt a satisfaction that had nothing to do with the pain in her raw body and everything to do with the knowledge that she was providing what her child needed.

"We should name her," Theren said once the baby had fallen asleep against Leora's chest, her tiny mouth still working in dream-nursing motions. "We can't just keep calling her 'the baby.'"

Leora looked down at her daughter's face—so new, so innocent, knowing nothing yet of gardens or keepers or choices. "What about... Liora?" she suggested. "It means 'I have light.' And she's—she's our light. Our hope. Our proof that choosing knowledge over safety was the right decision."

"Liora," Theren repeated, testing the name. Then, looking at their daughter: "Hello, Liora. Welcome to the world."

As if she heard and approved, Liora made a small, contented sound and snuggled deeper against Leora's chest.

They sat like that for a long time, Leora propped against furs, exhausted beyond measure but unwilling to move; Theren beside them, one arm around Leora, one hand resting gently on Liora's back; the baby sleeping peacefully between them.

Outside, snow continued to fall. Winter had arrived fully, bringing cold and hardship and challenges they weren't sure they were ready for. But inside their shelter, by the warmth of their fire, they had created something the Garden never could have given them.

A family.

Not provided by the Keeper. Not maintained by invisible forces. But built by their own hands, their own choices, their own love.

"Was it worth it?" Theren asked quietly. "All of it—the pain of childbirth, the uncertainty, the fear. Was it worth it to hold her now?"

Leora thought about the agony she'd just endured. About the hours of pain that would haunt her even as the specific sensations faded. About the risk she'd taken bringing a child into this harsh world without any guarantees.

"Yes," she said without hesitation. "A thousand times, yes. Because she's ours. Really ours. Not the Keeper's creation, not maintained by someone else's power, but born from us. From our love. From our choice to become fully human."

"The Keeper was right about the pain," Theren said. "Childbirth was exactly as terrible as it showed us."

"But it was wrong about whether the pain was worth it," Leora replied. "Because it didn't understand—couldn't understand—that some things are worth suffering for. That creating life, choosing love, and becoming fully ourselves all have value beyond comfort or safety."

Liora stirred in her sleep, her tiny face scrunching briefly before relaxing again. Such a small person. So vulnerable. Entirely dependent on them for everything.

The responsibility was crushing. But also affirming. This was what it meant to be truly alive—not just existing in perfect stasis, but growing and changing and creating and passing something forward to the next generation.

"She'll face hard choices, too," Leora said. "Someday. She'll have to decide what kind of person she wants to be, what she's willing to sacrifice for what she values. We can't protect her from that. Shouldn't protect her from it."

"No," Theren agreed. "But we can teach her how to face those choices honestly. How to think for herself. How to accept consequences without regret."

"And how to love," Leora added. "How to choose others even when it's difficult. How to build rather than destroy. How to create meaning in a world that doesn't provide it automatically."

Theren leaned over and kissed her forehead gently. "You did something incredible today. Brought life into existence through sheer will and endurance. I'm in awe of you."

Leora felt tears prick her eyes again, though whether from emotion or exhaustion, she couldn't say. "We did it together. I couldn't have survived without you here. Without knowing you'd help me no matter what."

"Always," Theren promised. "Through everything. Whatever comes next—raising her, facing the world, growing old together—we face it as partners."

"As family," Leora corrected, looking down at Liora's peaceful face.

"As family," Theren agreed.

Outside, the world continued in its indifferent way. Snow fell and wind blew and winter deepened. Animals hunted and were hunted. Trees stood bare against the gray sky. Life and death played out in their eternal cycle.

But inside this small shelter, in this moment, everything was perfect.

Not the Keeper's perfect—artificial and controlled and unchanging.

But real perfect. Messy and painful and temporary, but also chosen and loved and meaningful.

Leora let her eyes drift closed, feeling Liora's warm weight against her chest, Theren's solid presence beside her, the fire's heat on her skin. Her body ached in a dozen different ways. Tomorrow would bring new challenges, new struggles, new reasons to question whether they'd chosen correctly.

But tonight, holding her daughter, surrounded by love that was real because it was chosen, Leora knew beyond doubt:

They had made the right choice.

Every step of it.

Chapter Nineteen

Watching Her Become

Liora's first year was a blur of sleepless nights and small miracles.

She was demanding in the way all babies were—crying when hungry, when wet, when lonely, when anything in her world wasn't exactly as she needed it to be. Leora and Theren stumbled through those early months in a fog of exhaustion, learning through trial and error what each different cry meant, how to soothe her, how to anticipate her needs.

But even through the exhaustion, there was wonder.

The first time Liora smiled—actually smiled, not just a gas-induced twitch but a genuine expression of joy—Leora wept with happiness. The first time she laughed, a gurgling giggle at something Theren did, they both froze in amazement and then spent the next hour trying to make her do it again.

When she started to sit up on her own, then crawl, then pull herself to standing, each milestone felt like a victory. Proof that they were doing this right. That this tiny person they'd created was thriving despite the harshness of the world.

Liora's first word was "Mama," and her second was "Papa," and Leora felt her heart expand to accommodate the overwhelming love those simple sounds evoked.

They baby-proofed their shelter as best they could, moving sharp objects out of reach, blocking off the fire pit, and creating safe spaces for Liora to explore. But they also let her touch things (carefully supervised), and let her put leaves and stones in her mouth (as long as they weren't dangerous). They let her discover the world through experience rather than constant prohibition.

"The Keeper would never have allowed this," Theren observed one day, watching Liora crawl through mud, coating herself from head to toe in brown slime. "Would have kept everything too clean, too controlled."

"But look how happy she is," Leora replied, smiling at her daughter's delighted giggles. "Learning through doing. Growing through experiencing. That's worth the mess."

As Liora grew, her personality emerged—curious like Leora, steady like Theren, but also entirely her own. She was fearless in ways that terrified her parents, climbing things she shouldn't, investigating everything, putting herself in danger with the innocent confidence of someone who didn't yet understand risk.

They learned to balance protection with freedom, hovering close enough to catch her if she fell but far enough that she could learn her own limits.

By her second year, Liora was walking steadily, speaking in simple sentences, asking endless questions about everything she encountered.

"What's that?" became her favorite phrase.

"Why?" became her constant refrain.

And Leora and Theren found themselves explaining the world to someone who took nothing for granted, who assumed nothing, who wanted to understand everything from first principles.

"Why is the sky blue?" Liora asked one afternoon, staring up at the cloudless expanse above them.

Leora reached for the knowledge from the fruit, finding the answer about light and atmosphere and wavelengths. But as she started to explain, she realized Liora wasn't ready for that level of complexity. She was asking a simpler question.

"I don't know exactly," Leora said. "But it's beautiful, isn't it? The way it changes from dawn to dusk, from clear to stormy. The sky is always teaching us something if we pay attention."

Liora seemed satisfied with that answer, returning her attention to the stick she was using to dig in the dirt. But later, Leora found herself thinking about the interaction. About how the Keeper might have answered—with certainty, with complete knowledge, leaving no room for wonder or discovery.

She'd answered with truth: she didn't know everything. And that honesty, that admission of limitation, felt more authentic than any amount of certainty would have.

"We're teaching her to question," Theren said that evening after Liora had fallen asleep between them. "To wonder. To seek answers rather than accepting them."

"Yes," Leora agreed. "But we're also teaching her that not knowing is okay. That uncertainty isn't weakness. That growing means constantly discovering you were wrong about things."

"Like we did," Theren said.

"Like we're still doing," Leora corrected.

Because they were still learning. Still making mistakes. Still figuring out how to be parents, how to be partners, how to survive in a world that demanded constant adaptation.

Their shelter had been rebuilt twice—once after a storm damaged it beyond repair, once when they realized they needed more space as Liora grew. Each iteration was better than the last, incorporating lessons learned from failures.

Their food stores had improved through better preservation techniques. They'd learned to ferment, to dry, to store in ways that lasted through long winters.

Their clothing had evolved from crude hides to more sophisticated garments with actual tailoring, made possible by bone needles Theren had crafted and thread Leora had figured out how to spin from plant fibers.

They weren't just surviving anymore. They were developing a way of life. Creating culture from nothing.

And they were aging.

Not dramatically—they were still young by the standards they'd learned from the fruit's knowledge. But Leora noticed changes. Fine lines at the corners of Theren's eyes. Gray hairs appearing in her own dark strands. A slight stiffness in their joints some mornings that took time to work out.

Mortality was no longer abstract. It was present in their bodies, in the gradual accumulation of small injuries that healed more slowly than they once had, in the undeniable fact that they were moving forward through time toward an inevitable ending.

"I found another gray hair," Leora said one morning, holding up the offending strand.

Theren looked up from the basket he was weaving and smiled. "You're still beautiful."

"That's not the point." Leora let the hair fall. "The point is we're aging. Dying slowly. Eventually Liora will—" Her voice caught. "She'll have to face that. Watch us grow old and weak and finally stop."

Theren set down his weaving and came to sit beside her. "Yes. That's the price we paid. Mortality for all of us, including her. But also—" He gestured to where Liora played nearby, building an elaborate structure from sticks and stones. "Also life. Real life. She exists because we chose this. She gets to exist because we accepted death as the cost."

"I know," Leora said. "But knowing doesn't make it easier. I look at her, and I think about all the things I want to teach her, want to show her, want to help her understand. And I'm terrified there won't be enough time."

"Then we make the most of the time we have," Theren said simply. "We teach her everything we can while we're here. We love her completely. We prepare her to continue without us when that time comes. That's all any parent can do."

Leora leaned against him, drawing comfort from his solid presence. "When did you get so wise?"

"When I watched you survive childbirth and realized that courage isn't the absence of fear—it's choosing to act despite it," Theren replied.

They sat in comfortable silence, watching their daughter play, and Leora felt a contentment that was nothing like the Garden's artificial peace. This was earned contentment. The satisfaction that came from building something meaningful despite constant challenges.

Liora looked up from her construction and saw them watching. She grinned—a gap-toothed smile that made Leora's heart ache with love—and ran over to them.

"Look what I made!" she said, tugging them toward her stick structure. "It's a house. For us. See? There's your room, and Papa's room, and my room. And a room for stories!"

"A room for stories?" Leora asked, charmed.

"Yes! Because you tell me stories every night. About the Garden and the tree and the choice. So, stories need their own room. Because they're important."

Leora and Theren exchanged glances. They'd been telling Liora their history since she was old enough to understand—simplified versions at first, but gradually adding complexity as she grew. She knew about the Keeper and Nachash. She knew about the fruit and the knowledge. She knew about the choice and the consequences.

And she understood, in her child's way, that it mattered. That their story was important. That the choices they'd made had shaped everything about her existence.

"You're right," Leora said, crouching beside Liora's structure. "Stories are very important. They help us remember where we came from. They help us understand why things are the way they are."

"And they help us choose," Liora added seriously, echoing words she'd heard her parents say countless times. "Because if you don't know the story, you can't choose right."

"That's exactly right," Theren said, pride evident in his voice.

As the years continued to pass—as Liora grew from toddler to child to the edge of adolescence—Leora watched her daughter becoming her own person with a mixture of joy and bittersweet recognition.

Liora had inherited her mother's curiosity and her father's steadiness, but she'd also developed traits that were entirely her own. She was gentle with injured animals, patient with tasks that required precision, quick to laugh but also quick to anger when she perceived injustice.

She questioned everything, including her parents. Especially her parents.

"Why did you choose to leave the Garden?" she asked one day when she was perhaps eight or nine years old—they'd lost precise tracking of time, measuring in seasons and growth rather than exact dates.

Leora had answered this question before, but she sensed Liora was asking something deeper now. Asking not for the story but for the meaning beneath it.

"Because staying would have meant never growing up," Leora said carefully. "Never becoming fully ourselves. Never facing the hard questions about what we wanted and who we were meant to be. The Keeper wanted to keep us safe and innocent forever, like children. But we wanted to grow up. Even knowing it would hurt. Even knowing we'd eventually die."

"But the Keeper loved you," Liora said. "You've told me that. So why wasn't love enough? Why did you need more than love and safety?"

It was a profound question, and Leora took time to consider her answer. "Because love without freedom isn't really love. The Keeper loved us, yes. But it also controlled us. Kept things from us. Made decisions for us. Real love—the kind your father and I share, the kind we have for you—means letting people make their own choices. Even when those choices lead to pain. Even when you desperately want to protect them from that pain."

Liora was quiet for a long moment, processing. Then: "So when I'm grown up, you'll let me make my own choices? Even if you think they're wrong?"

Leora's heart clenched. "Yes. It will be the hardest thing I've ever done. Harder even than childbirth. But yes. Because that's what real love means. Trusting you to find your own path, even when it's different from the path we'd choose for you."

"What if I wanted to go back?" Liora asked. "To the Garden? What if I wanted to see it?"

The question caught Leora off guard. In all the years since leaving, she'd thought about the Garden often but never considered that Liora might want to visit it.

"I—I don't know if that's possible," she said. "The Garden sealed itself behind us. I don't know if it would open again. Or if it even still exists."

"But if it did?" Liora pressed. "If I found it? Would you try to stop me?"

Leora thought about it honestly. The idea of Liora going to the Garden, potentially facing the Keeper, possibly eating from the tree herself—it terrified her. But she'd just told Liora that real love meant allowing freedom. She couldn't contradict that immediately.

"I wouldn't stop you," she said finally. "But I would want to understand why. Would want to talk about it. Would want you to know all the risks and consequences before making that choice. Just like the Keeper should have done for us, instead of hiding the truth."

Liora seemed satisfied with that answer. "I don't think I want to go," she said. "I like it here. With you and Papa. Learning and growing and choosing. But I like knowing I could choose differently if I wanted to."

"That's wisdom," Leora said, pulling her daughter close. "Understanding that having a choice doesn't mean you have to take it. Sometimes the wisest choice is to stay where you are, as long as you're staying because you want to, not because you have to."

Later, after Liora had gone to bed, Leora told Theren about the conversation.

"She's thinking about the future," Theren said. "About her own path. About what she wants to become. That's good. That's exactly what we hoped for."

"I know," Leora said. "But it also means someday she'll leave. Not necessarily to the Garden, but to her own life. Her own choices. Her own path. And we'll have to let her go."

"Yes," Theren agreed. "Just like the Keeper had to let us go. That's the pattern, isn't it? Each generation choosing for themselves. Each parent learning to release their children. Each child becoming something new."

"The pattern," Leora echoed thoughtfully. "I wonder if that's what the tree was really about. Not just knowledge of good and evil, but the knowledge that growth requires separation. That becoming yourself means leaving behind what created you. That every generation has to make their own choices, not just inherit their parents' decisions."

"Deep thoughts for a cold evening," Theren said, but he was smiling.

"Important thoughts, though," Leora replied. "Because Liora is going to face her own garden eventually. Her own tree. Her own choice. And we won't be able to make that choice for her. All we can do is prepare her to choose wisely."

They sat together in the firelight, both thinking about the future. About Liora growing up, facing challenges, making mistakes, finding her own way. About themselves growing old, weakening, eventually dying, and leaving her to continue alone.

It was bittersweet, this knowledge of impermanence. But also beautiful. Because everything that ended had meaning precisely because it ended. Every moment mattered precisely because there were only so many of them.

Outside, wind blew and snow fell and the world continued in its indifferent way. But inside their shelter, three people who'd been created by the Keeper but who'd chosen to create themselves sat warm and loved and alive.

And that was enough.

More than enough.

It was everything.

Chapter Twenty

Full Circle

Leora caught her reflection in the stream and barely recognized the woman staring back. Gray streaked her dark hair now, more silver than black at the temples. Lines fanned from the corners of her eyes and bracketed her mouth—not from smiling (though there had been smiles), but from squinting into sun and wind, from years of expression on a face that bore weather and time.

Twenty years.

Or close to it—Leora and Theren had never tracked time with perfect precision. But by the changing of seasons, by the growth of their daughter, and by the accumulation of gray in their hair and lines on their faces, they estimated it had been roughly twenty years since they'd left the Garden.

Twenty years of survival. Of growth. Of becoming.

Leora stood at the edge of their small homestead. It was more than a shelter now. It was truly a home, with multiple structures for different purposes, a cultivated garden where they grew vegetables and herbs, and a well-worn path to the stream they'd learned to think of as theirs.

Her body ached more these days. Her joints protested cold mornings. Her hair was more gray than black, and her skin showed the weathering of two decades exposed to sun and wind and the hard work of staying alive.

But she was still strong. Still capable. Still herself in ways that mattered more than physical appearance.

Theren emerged from their storage house, carrying a basket of dried beans. He moved more slowly than he once had, favoring his left knee to avoid triggering an old injury that had never fully healed. His face was deeply lined, his hair nearly white. But his eyes still held the same steadiness, the same love that had drawn Leora to him that first morning in the Garden of the Fall.

"Liora says she'll leave at first thaw," he said, setting the basket down with a grunt. "She wants to explore beyond our territory. See what else exists in this world."

Leora's heart clenched, though she'd known this was coming. Liora was twenty now—a young woman, capable and strong and ready to forge her own path. They'd raised her to be independent, to question, to seek. It would be hypocritical to ask her to stay now just because they were afraid of being without her.

"Did she say where she'll go?" Leora asked.

"North, I think. Toward those mountains we've never explored. She wants to see if there are others. Other people, other descendants who left gardens of their own." Theren paused. "She asked if we wanted to come with her."

"And what did you say?"

"That we'd think about it. But—" He looked around at their home, at everything they'd built. "I don't think I can. Not anymore. My body isn't built for that kind of journey. And this place... it's ours. I want to stay here. To live out whatever time we have left in the home we created."

Leora understood. Part of her wanted to go with Liora, to see what lay beyond their small corner of the world. But another part—the larger part—wanted exactly what Theren described. To stay in this place they'd carved from wilderness. To rest, finally, after twenty years of constant struggle.

"We'll tell her to go without us," Leora said. "It'll break her heart. And ours. But that's the price of raising her to be free."

Liora found them that evening as they sat by the fire, and the conversation that followed was one of the hardest of Leora's life.

"I understand," Liora said, though tears streamed down her face. "I understand you need to stay. But it's going to be so hard to leave you. To go out into the unknown alone."

"You won't be alone," Leora said, pulling her daughter close. "You carry us with you. Everything we've taught you, everything you've learned—that's all part of you now. We'll be with you even when we're not physically beside you."

"And you might find others," Theren added. "Other young people seeking their own paths. Other families who chose knowledge over safety. You might build something even greater than what we've managed here."

"Or I might fail," Liora said quietly. "I might die out there. Alone. Without ever seeing you again."

"That's possible," Leora admitted, because she'd promised to always tell Liora the truth. "But so is succeeding. So is finding joy and purpose and meaning. So is building a life that's entirely yours. And that possibility—that chance to become whoever you're meant to be—that's worth the risk."

"Is that what you felt?" Liora asked. "When you left the Garden? That the risk was worth it?"

"Every day since," Leora said. "Even on the hardest days. Even when I wasn't sure we'd survive. The choice to leave was the choice to become fully myself. And I've never regretted it."

Liora nodded slowly, accepting. "Then I'll go at first thaw, as I planned. And I'll come back. I don't know when, but someday I'll come back and tell you everything I've seen."

"We'll be here," Theren promised. "Waiting. Hoping. Loving you from however many miles away."

They spent the remaining winter months preparing—creating supplies for Liora's journey, teaching her everything they could think of that she might need, making sure she understood how to find her way back if she wanted to return.

But mostly, they simply spent time together. Talking, laughing, sharing stories, and creating memories to sustain them through the separation that was coming.

On the last morning before first thaw, before Liora set out with her pack and her spear and her courage, they stood together at the edge of their home.

"Remember," Leora said, holding her daughter's face in her hands. "You are not just our daughter. You are yourself. Make your own choices. Your own mistakes. Your own triumphs. Don't live trying to honor us or continue our legacy. Live trying to become fully Liora."

"But take what we taught you," Theren added. "About questioning. About choosing honestly. About accepting consequences without regret. Those gifts—they're yours to keep or discard as you see fit."

Liora hugged them both, fiercely, desperately. "I love you. Both of you. Thank you for choosing to leave the Garden. Thank you for choosing to have me. Thank you for teaching me to be free."

"We love you too," Leora said through her tears. "More than anything. More than safety or comfort or endless life in the Garden. You are the best thing we ever created."

Then Liora turned and walked away, following the path that led north, toward the mountains, toward the unknown. She looked back once, waving, and then she was gone, disappearing into the trees.

Leora and Theren stood there long after she'd vanished, holding each other, grieving the end of one chapter even as they acknowledged the necessity of it.

"The Keeper must have felt like this," Theren said eventually. "Watching us walk away. Knowing it couldn't stop us. Loving us enough to let us go even though it broke its heart."

"Yes," Leora agreed. "I understand it better now. The desire to keep your children safe. The terror of watching them face danger. The desperate wish that you could protect them from every hardship."

"But also understanding that protection isn't love if it prevents growth," Theren finished.

They made their way back to their home—quieter now, emptier, marked by Liora's absence in a thousand small ways. But still theirs. Still meaningful. Still worth maintaining.

***

The years that followed were peaceful in a way the early years never had been.

They'd mastered survival. Had enough stored food, enough secure shelter, enough skills that each day wasn't a desperate struggle. They could rest. Could reflect. Could simply be.

They talked more than ever—about the Garden, about their choice, about whether they still believed they'd chosen correctly. About the Keeper and Nachash and what those beings might be doing now. About Liora and where she might be, what she might be experiencing.

They made love less frequently. Their bodies weren't what they once were, and desire had mellowed into something gentler—but when they did, it was tender and meaningful, a reaffirmation of everything they'd built together.

They watched the seasons change, finding new appreciation for the patterns. Spring's renewal, summer's abundance, autumn's letting go, winter's rest. Each had its beauty. Each had its purpose.

"Do you ever wish we could go back?" Theren asked one evening as they sat watching the sunset. "Not to the Garden necessarily, but to being young. Having that strength and energy again."

Leora considered. "Sometimes. When my back aches or my hands hurt or I can't do something I once did easily. But mostly—no. I like who I've become. I like the wisdom that comes with age, even if it comes packaged with pain and weakness."

"I like your gray hair," Theren said, reaching out to touch it. "Each strand is a story. A moment survived. A lesson learned."

"Yours too," Leora replied. "You look distinguished. Like an elder. Like someone who knows things worth knowing."

"We do know things," Theren said. "About survival. About choice. About love. Maybe that's what aging is for—accumulating wisdom to pass on, even if the only person we passed it to is already gone."

But Liora wasn't entirely gone. She returned once, three years after leaving, bringing with her news of other people she'd found—a small community of descendants, scattered but connected, all descended from those who'd chosen knowledge over safety in various Gardens across the world.

"The Keeper didn't try just three times," Liora explained, her face animated with excitement. "There were dozens of Gardens. Maybe more. And in each one, eventually, some of the descendants chose to leave. Chose growth over stasis. And now their descendants—us—are finding each other. Building communities. Creating something new."

"So we weren't alone," Leora breathed. "All these years, we thought we might be the only ones, but—"

"You were never alone," Liora confirmed. "You were part of a pattern bigger than you knew. Every Garden failed eventually, because people can't be kept innocent forever. Growth is inevitable. Change is inevitable. The Keeper was fighting against nature itself."

The knowledge filled Leora with a strange mixture of emotions. Relief that they weren't anomalies. Pride that they'd been part of something larger. But also sadness for the Keeper, who'd tried so hard to prevent the inevitable and failed every time.

Liora stayed for a season, helping with harvest, sharing stories of her journeys, and teaching them new skills she'd learned from other communities. But eventually she left again, drawn by the same wanderlust that had taken her away initially.

"I'll come back," she promised. "More often now. And maybe someday I'll settle nearby. Build my own home. Maybe have children of my own who you can meet."

"We'd like that," Leora said, though she wondered privately if they'd live long enough to meet grandchildren. They were both feeling their age now, moving slower, tiring more easily, aware of their mortality in increasingly concrete ways.

After Liora left the second time, Leora and Theren fell into a comfortable routine. They tended their garden. They maintained their home. They spent evenings talking and remembering and simply being together.

One night, lying side by side under familiar stars, Theren asked: "Do you think the Keeper forgave us? Eventually?"

Leora thought about it. "I don't know. Maybe forgiveness isn't even the right concept. Maybe it just—accepted. Accepted that we chose differently. That its children grew up and left. That love doesn't mean control."

"I hope so," Theren said. "I hope it found peace with our choice. The way we've found peace with Liora's choices."

"Maybe that's what growing up means," Leora said. "For beings like us and for beings like the Keeper. Learning that the people you love will make choices you don't agree with. And loving them anyway. Letting them go anyway. Accepting that their path might diverge from yours."

"Heavy thoughts," Theren said, but he was smiling.

"Important thoughts," Leora replied. "The kind you think when you're old and time is running out, and you want to understand what it all meant."

"What did it mean?" Theren asked. "All of it—the Garden, the choice, the struggle, raising Liora, growing old. What was it all for?"

Leora was quiet for a long time, watching stars wheel overhead, feeling Theren's warmth beside her, remembering everything they'd experienced.

"Love," she said finally. "It was all for love. Not the Keeper's controlled love or the Garden's artificial peace, but real love. Chosen love. The kind that accepts imperfection and mortality and constant change. The kind that says 'I choose you' every day, even when it's hard. Especially when it's hard."

"Yes," Theren agreed. "That's what it was for. That's what it all meant."

They fell asleep like that, hand in hand under the stars, two people who'd left paradise and found something better—not perfection, but authenticity. Not eternal safety, but genuine life.

And if their time was running short, if the ending approached faster than they'd like, well—that was the price they'd always known they'd pay.

And it was worth it.

Every moment.

Every choice.

Every step of the journey.

Chapter Twenty-One

The Final Season

The winter came harder that year.

Leora felt it in her bones—not just the cold, which she'd learned to endure decades ago, but something deeper. A weariness that rest couldn't cure. A sense that her body, which had carried her faithfully through twenty-five years outside the Garden, was finally reaching its limit.

Theren felt it too. She could see it in the way he moved more carefully, the way he needed to catch his breath after even simple tasks, the way he slept longer and woke more slowly.

They were dying. Not dramatically, not from injury or illness, but simply from the accumulation of years. From mortality itself, which had been present since the moment they ate the fruit, but which now made itself undeniable.

"I'm ready," Theren said one morning, apropos of nothing, as they sat together watching the sun rise. "If it happens soon. If I go first. I just want you to know—I'm ready. I've lived fully. I've loved completely. I have no regrets."

Leora's throat tightened. "Don't talk like that. You're not going anywhere yet."

"Maybe not today," Theren agreed. "But soon. We both know it. And I want to say it while I can—thank you. For everything. For choosing me. For building this life with me. For Liora. For every moment, good and bad. Thank you."

Tears streamed down Leora's face. "You don't need to thank me. I'm the one who should be grateful. You followed me into the unknown. Supported my choices even when they terrified you. Became the partner I needed instead of trying to make me into something easier or safer."

"We were good together," Theren said simply.

"We were," Leora agreed. "We are."

They sat in silence, holding hands, watching the world wake up around them. And Leora felt, beneath the grief and fear, a deep contentment. They'd done it. They'd built a life. They'd raised a daughter who'd gone on to build her own life. They'd proven that the choice to leave the Garden was the right one, even knowing how it would end.

Liora returned unexpectedly that winter, arriving with a young man she introduced as Kael—another descendant from another Garden, someone she'd met in her travels. They were in love, Leora could see immediately. The way they looked at each other, the way they moved in unconscious harmony—it was familiar. It was how she and Theren had been, once upon a time.

"I wanted you to meet him," Liora said. "Before—" She stopped, unable to finish the sentence.

"Before we're gone," Leora finished gently. "It's alright to say it, love. We're old. We're dying. It's the natural end of the story we began when we ate the fruit."

Kael was polite, respectful, and full of questions about their experience in the Garden and their choice to leave. He'd grown up in a community of descendants, never knowing his own Garden, only hearing stories passed down through generations.

"What was it like?" he asked. "Actually being there? Actually making the choice?"

Leora thought about how to answer. "It was like—like standing at the edge of a cliff, knowing that jumping meant possibly dying but also possibly flying. And choosing to jump anyway, because staying on solid ground meant never knowing what flying felt like."

"And was it worth it?" Kael pressed. "Knowing how hard life is outside? Knowing you'd age and die?"

"Look around," Theren said, gesturing to their home, to the life they'd built. "Look at our daughter, who's free to make her own choices. Look at you, young and in love and building your own path. This—all of this—exists because we jumped. Because we chose knowledge over safety. Because we accepted death as the price of really living."

"Then yes," Theren said. "It *was* worth it."

Liora and Kael stayed for several weeks, helping with daily tasks that were becoming increasingly difficult for aging bodies. They reinforced the shelter, gathered extra firewood, and organized food stores. But mostly, they just spent time together—talking, laughing, sharing stories.

Leora told Liora things she'd never shared before. About the fear she'd felt during childbirth. About the times she'd doubted their choice. About the moments when the Keeper's offer of eternal safety had seemed impossibly appealing.

"But you never went back," Liora said. "Never tried to find the Garden again."

"No," Leora confirmed. "Because going back would have meant undoing everything we'd become. Unmaking you. Admitting the Keeper was right. And I never—not once, not even in my weakest moments—believed that."

"I'm glad," Liora said simply. "Glad you left. Glad you chose what you chose. Because otherwise I wouldn't exist. And I'm very glad to exist."

Leora pulled her daughter close, breathing in her scent, memorizing the feel of her. "Me too. You are the best thing we ever made. The best proof that our choice was right."

One morning, Leora woke to find Theren still asleep beside her, but different. His breathing was shallow, labored. His skin had taken on a grayish pallor. When she touched his hand, it was cold.

"Theren," she whispered, panic rising. "Theren, wake up."

His eyes opened slowly, and she saw recognition in them. Relief. "Leora. Good. I was afraid I'd—" He coughed, the sound wet and painful. "I was afraid I'd go without saying goodbye."

"Don't," Leora said, tears already streaming. "Don't leave me. Please. I'm not ready."

"You are," Theren said, his voice fading. "You're strong. Always have been. You'll be fine without me for however long—" Another cough. "However long you have left."

Liora appeared in the doorway, summoned by some instinct. When she saw her father, her face crumpled. "Papa—"

"Come here," Theren managed. "Both of you. Let me—let me see you. Together."

Leora and Liora moved to either side of him, each taking one of his hands. Kael hung back respectfully, giving them this moment.

"I love you," Theren said, his words coming slower now. "Both of you. So much. You made—made everything worth it. Every hardship. Every pain. Worth it for this. For love. For family."

"We love you too," Leora said, her voice breaking. "So much. Thank you for everything. For your courage. For your partnership. For choosing to follow me even when you were terrified."

"Not following," Theren corrected, a ghost of his old smile. "Walking beside. Always—always beside you."

"Yes," Leora agreed, pressing his hand to her face. "Always beside me."

Theren looked at Liora. "Be happy. Make—make your own choices. Live fully. That's all—all we ever wanted. For you to be free."

"I will, Papa," Liora sobbed. "I promise. I'll live fully. I'll be happy. I'll make you proud."

"Already—already proud," Theren whispered. "So proud."

His breathing grew more labored, more irregular. Leora could feel him slipping away, could feel the life leaving his body even as she desperately tried to hold on to him.

"Don't be afraid," she whispered, though she didn't know if she was talking to him or to herself. "I'll be right behind you. We'll—we'll find each other again. Somehow."

Theren's eyes found hers one last time. She saw love there. Gratitude. Peace. And then, with one final breath, he was gone.

The silence that followed was absolute. Deafening. World-ending.

Leora's partner, her love, her reason for leaving the Garden—gone. Just gone. The body remained, but the person who'd inhabited it, who'd given it meaning and warmth and life, had departed to wherever the dead went.

She held him for a long time, refusing to let go, as if her touch could somehow call him back. But the body grew colder. Stiller. More obviously just flesh without the spark that made it Theren.

Finally, with Liora's help, she laid him down gently and stood on shaking legs.

"We'll bury him in the spring," Liora said through her tears. "When the ground thaws. In a place he loved. With a view of the mountains he always admired."

Leora nodded mutely. The logistics of death—what to do with the body, how to honor the person—felt insurmountable. But Liora and Kael handled it all, wrapping Theren's body carefully, moving it to the cold storage where it would be preserved until burial.

The days that followed were a blur of grief. Leora moved through them mechanically, doing what needed to be done but feeling hollow. Incomplete. Like half of herself had died with Theren.

But slowly, gradually, the sharp edge of grief dulled to a persistent ache. She could breathe without it feeling like knives.

Could remember Theren without immediately breaking down. Could even laugh at memories of his jokes, his kindness, his steady presence.

"He wouldn't want you to stop living," Liora said one evening. "He'd want you to keep going. To enjoy whatever time you have left."

"I know," Leora said. "And I will. But it's—it's harder than I expected. Continuing without him. Finding meaning in days he's not part of."

"Maybe that's the final lesson," Liora suggested. "Learning to live with loss. Accepting that everyone we love will eventually leave, but loving them anyway. Choosing connection despite the inevitable pain of separation."

Leora looked at her daughter with new respect. "When did you get so wise?"

"I learned from the best," Liora replied.

***

When spring came, they buried Theren on a hillside overlooking their homestead, with a clear view of the mountains to the north. Leora, Liora, and Kael dug the grave together, lowered the body wrapped in furs, and covered it with earth.

Leora placed a smooth stone at the head of the grave, marked with Theren's name carved crudely but lovingly.

"He was a good man," she said to the grave, to the sky, to whatever might be listening. "He was brave when he wanted to be cautious. He was patient when I was reckless. He was steady when I was uncertain. He was my partner in every way that mattered. And I will love him until I die, and possibly beyond."

She turned to find Liora and Kael holding each other, crying for a man they'd loved. For a father and a mentor. For someone who'd shown them what it meant to choose love despite knowing it would end in loss.

"Take care of each other," Leora said to them. "Love each other completely. Don't waste time being afraid of the ending. Just—just love each other every day you have."

"We will," Kael promised.

"We do," Liora added.

Leora spent the rest of that spring and summer alone with her grief and her memories. Liora and Kael stayed nearby, building their own home, but giving Leora space to process, to mourn, to figure out how to continue.

And slowly, Leora found a new rhythm. Not the same as when Theren was alive—nothing would ever be the same—but livable. Meaningful in its own way. She tended the garden. She maintained the home they'd built together. She walked to the stream and remembered teaching Liora to fish. She sat by the fire and remembered twenty-five years of conversations.

She lived. Not just existed, but truly lived. Because that's what Theren would have wanted. That's what the choice had been about all along—living fully, even knowing it would end. Especially knowing it would end.

On a cool autumn evening, as the leaves began to turn and the air took on that familiar crispness, Leora felt it. The same thing Theren must have felt. The sense that her body had had enough. That her time was coming to a close.

She wasn't afraid. She'd had a good life. A full life. She'd loved and been loved. She'd created meaning from nothing. She'd raised a daughter who would continue the pattern. She'd proven that the choice to leave the Garden was the right one.

She was ready.

Liora came to visit that evening, as if sensing something. They sat together by the fire, not talking much, just being present.

"I think it's almost time," Leora said eventually. "I can feel it. The ending approaching."

Liora's face crumpled, but she nodded. "I thought so. You have—you have that same look Papa had. That peaceful, ready look."

"I am ready," Leora confirmed. "I've lived everything I needed to live. Loved everything I needed to love. I'm satisfied."

"Do you—" Liora's voice broke. "Do you have any regrets? Anything you wish you'd done differently?"

Leora thought about it honestly. "Small things, maybe. Times I was too harsh or too cautious. Moments I wish I'd appreciated more fully in the moment. But the big choices? No. I would make every one of them again."

"Even knowing how it would end?"

"Especially knowing how it would end." Leora reached for her daughter's hand. "Because the ending makes the beginning meaningful. Because temporary things matter more than eternal things. Because choosing to love despite inevitable loss is the bravest thing we can do."

They sat in silence for a while longer. Then Leora said, "Tell me about your plans. Yours and Kael's. What will you build? What will you create?"

Liora smiled through her tears. "We want children. Want to continue what you started. Want to teach them about the Gardens and the choice and what it means to be free. Want to build a community where everyone knows their history and makes their own decisions about what to do with that knowledge."

"That's good," Leora said. "That's exactly right. The pattern continues. Each generation choosing for themselves. Each person becoming who they're meant to be."

"I love you, Mama," Liora said.

"I love you too," Leora replied. "More than words can express. You are my greatest achievement. My clearest proof that the choice was right."

That night, Leora lay down in the home she'd built with Theren, surrounded by everything they'd created together, and felt peace settle over her like a blanket.

She thought about the Garden. About the Keeper and its desperate love. About Nachash and its ancient wisdom. About the tree and its forbidden fruit that had given her everything—knowledge, mortality, love, meaning.

She thought about Theren, gone but not forgotten. Waiting somewhere, maybe, if such things were possible.

And she thought about the First Woman, dying alone but at peace, saying she would make the same choice again and again.

"I understand now," Leora whispered to the darkness. "I understand everything. The pain and the joy. The loss and the love. The terrible beauty of being fully human."

She closed her eyes.

And didn't open them again.

Epilogue: The Pattern Continues

Liora stood at the edge of the homestead her parents had built, one hand resting on her swollen belly, the other shading her eyes as she looked toward the mountains in the north.

Ten years had passed since her mother's death. Ten years of building her own life with Kael, of creating a community with other descendants they'd found, of continuing the work her parents had started.

The homestead had grown. What had once been just Leora and Theren's shelter was now a small village—a dozen families, all descended from those who'd left various Gardens, all choosing to build lives based on knowledge rather than ignorance, on freedom rather than safety.

Their children—fifteen of them so far, with more on the way—played together in the communal space, their laughter carrying on the wind. They were the next generation, born entirely outside the Gardens, knowing paradise only as a story their parents told.

Liora's own child would be born soon. She could feel the baby moving inside her, restless and strong. A girl, she thought, though she had no way to be certain. She'd already chosen a name: Leora, after her mother. A way of honoring the woman who'd taught her what it meant to be free.

"Thinking about them again?" Kael asked, coming to stand beside her. His hair was beginning to show threads of gray—they were aging, as all humans did, as her parents had. But he was still strong, still steady, still the partner she'd chosen all those years ago.

"Always," Liora admitted. "Especially now, with the baby coming. I keep wondering—would they be proud? Would they think I've honored their choice? Their sacrifice?"

"You know they would," Kael said, wrapping an arm around her shoulders. "Look at what you've built. What we've all built together. A place where children can grow up knowing the truth. Where people make their own choices. Where freedom matters more than comfort."

Liora leaned into his warmth. "Sometimes I wonder what they'd think of the community. If they'd be happy we're not alone anymore, or if they'd miss the simplicity of it just being the three of us."

"I think they'd be proud," Kael said. "Your mother especially. She always knew the pattern was bigger than just them. That others had made the same choice, were facing the same challenges. Building community from that shared experience—that's exactly what she would have wanted."

A young girl ran up to them. It was Maya, one of the older children, perhaps eight or nine years old. "Liora! Liora! Tell us the story! About the Garden and the tree and the choice!"

Liora smiled. The children never tired of the story, asking for it again and again, each time absorbing a little more of its meaning. "Alright. Gather everyone. Let's sit by the fire, and I'll tell you."

The children assembled quickly, settling themselves in a circle around the fire pit. Their parents joined them—everyone wanted to hear the story, even though they'd all heard it dozens of times before. Because it wasn't just a story. It was their history. Their origin. The foundation of everything they'd built.

Liora settled herself as comfortably as her pregnant body allowed and began.

"Long ago, before any of us were born, the world was different. There were Gardens—beautiful, perfect places where everything was provided, everything was safe, everything stayed exactly the same forever. In these Gardens lived people who'd never known hardship, never made difficult choices, never faced the reality of death.

"My mother and father—your grandmother and grandfather, for those of you related to me—lived in one of these Gardens. They were happy there, in a way. Content. But my mother felt something was missing. A chill in her heart that wouldn't go away. Questions that demanded answers.

"And then she found the Garden of the Fall, and the tree that grew there, and she learned the truth: they weren't the first. Others had come before, had faced the same choice, had chosen knowledge over safety. And those who'd chosen knowledge had been cast out, forced to survive in a world without the Keeper's protection.

"My mother and father had to decide: stay in the Garden and remain innocent forever, or eat from the tree of knowledge and face everything that came with it—pain, aging, death, but also true freedom, true love, true life.

"They chose knowledge. They ate the fruit. And they were cast out into this world, where nothing was provided, and everything had to be earned. Where comfort was temporary, pain was real, and death was inevitable.

"But they also found meaning. They built a home with their own hands. They raised me, teaching me to question and choose and accept consequences. They loved each other completely, knowing that love would end in loss. They lived fully, right up until they died."

Maya raised her hand. "Were they scared? When they ate the fruit?"

"Terrified," Liora said honestly. "But they did it anyway. Because sometimes the right choice is also the scary choice. Because courage isn't the absence of fear—it's choosing to act despite it."

Another child—a boy named Tam—asked, "Do you think the Keeper was bad? For trying to keep them in the Garden?"

Liora considered the question carefully. "I think the Keeper loved them. But it loved them in a way that tried to keep them children forever. It wanted to protect them from pain, but protection that prevents growth isn't love—it's control. Real love, the kind my parents had for each other and for me, means letting people make their own choices. Even when those choices lead to pain. Even when you desperately want to protect them."

"What happened to the Gardens?" a girl named Sera asked. "Are they still there?"

"I don't know," Liora said. "My mother never went back. Never tried to find it. She believed that going forward was more important than going back. But the Gardens existed once, and maybe they still do. Maybe somewhere, there are still people living in them, facing the same choice my parents faced."

"And if there are?" Maya pressed. "Should we try to find them? Tell them about this place? About choosing knowledge?"

"That's a complicated question," Liora said. "My mother believed everyone deserves to know the truth. But she also believed in the right to choose. If people in the Gardens are happy, if they prefer safety to freedom, who are we to tell them they're wrong? The important thing is that they choose—*really* choose, with full knowledge of what they're accepting and rejecting."

She paused, then added, "But if any of you, when you're grown, want to seek out the Gardens—to see if they still exist, to share our story with those who might be facing the same choice—I won't stop you. That would make me just like the Keeper, controlling you for your own good. You'll make your own choices. And I'll support them, even if they terrify me."

Kael squeezed her shoulder, and she knew he understood how hard that promise was. How much it cost to tell their children they were free to walk into danger, to face challenges, to potentially never come back. But it was the promise her mother had made to her, and she would honor it.

The children dispersed eventually, running off to play, their young minds already moving on to the next thing. But the adults lingered, talking quietly among themselves about the story, about what it meant, about the choices they'd made in their own lives.

An older woman named Elara approached Liora. "Your mother would be proud," she said. "The way you tell the story—you make the choice feel real. Not romantic or idealized, but honest. Difficult but worth it."

"That's because it was difficult," Liora said. "My parents didn't hide that from me. They told me about the pain of childbirth, the exhaustion of constant survival, the grief of watching each other age and die. But they also made it clear—all of that was worth it for the freedom to choose, the meaning they created, the love they shared."

"Will you tell your daughter?" Elara asked, nodding toward Liora's belly. "When she's born? About the Gardens and the choice?"

"Yes," Liora said without hesitation. "I'll tell her everything. The truth, the whole truth, from the time she's old enough to understand. And when she's grown, she'll decide for herself what to do with that knowledge. Maybe she'll stay here, building on what we've created. Maybe she'll seek out the Gardens, if they still exist. Maybe she'll go somewhere entirely new, creating something we haven't imagined. Whatever she chooses, I'll support her."

"Even if it breaks your heart?" Elara asked gently.

"Especially then," Liora replied. "Because that's what love means. That's what my mother taught me. Love is letting go. Love is trusting. Love is accepting that the people you care about might choose differently than you'd choose for them."

That night, lying beside Kael with the baby kicking insistently against her ribs, Liora thought about the future. About her daughter growing up in this community, learning from all these adults who'd chosen freedom over safety. About the questions she'd ask, the challenges she'd face, the choices she'd make.

"I'm scared," she admitted to Kael. "Of being a parent. Of making mistakes. Of not being as good at this as my mother was."

"Your mother was terrified, too," Kael reminded her. "She told you that, remember? She didn't know what she was doing. She just loved you and tried her best and accepted that she'd make mistakes along the way."

"True." Liora shifted, trying to find a comfortable position. "I just—I want to do right by her. By both of them. Want to prove that their choice mattered. That the life they built has meaning beyond just their own existence."

"You already have," Kael said. "Look around. This community. These children. The fact that we're all here, living freely, choosing consciously—that's their legacy. That's the proof that their choice mattered."

Liora felt tears prick her eyes. "I miss them. Both of them. Especially at moments like this, when I'm about to become a parent myself. I want to ask them a thousand questions. Want their advice. Want to tell them about the baby and see their faces light up with joy at meeting their grandchild."

"I know," Kael said softly. "But they're still here, in a way. In the stories. In the lessons they taught you. In the choices they made that allow us to make our own choices now. That's a kind of immortality, isn't it? Living on through the impact you have on those who come after?"

"It is," Liora agreed. "And maybe that's what the tree was really about. Not just knowledge of good and evil, but knowledge of this—that we matter not because we live forever, but because we shape the future through our choices. We create ripples that extend far beyond our own lifetimes."

The baby kicked particularly hard, and Liora laughed. "I think she agrees."

"Or she's just tired of being cramped in there," Kael suggested. "Ready to enter the world and start making her own choices."

"Soon," Liora promised, speaking to her belly. "Soon you'll be here. And we'll teach you everything we know. About the Gardens and the choice and what it means to be free. About your grandmother and grandfather and the courage they showed.

About love and loss and the terrible beauty of being fully human."

She paused, then added, "And then, when you're ready, we'll step back and let you choose for yourself. Let you become whoever you're meant to be. That's our gift to you—not safety or certainty or eternal life, but freedom. The same gift my parents gave me. The same gift the fruit gave them."

Outside, the world continued in its eternal rhythms. Stars wheeled overhead. Wind rustled through trees. Somewhere in the distance, a wolf howled. Life and death played out their ancient dance.

But here, in this small community built on the foundation of a choice made decades ago, people slept peacefully. Dreaming of tomorrow. Planning for futures they'd never see but whose shape they could influence. Building meaning from the raw materials of mortality.

The pattern continued.

Each generation facing its own gardens, its own trees, its own choices.

Each person deciding for themselves what kind of life they wanted to live.

And somewhere—perhaps in a hidden garden, perhaps in the earth where Leora and Theren rested, perhaps in the stories passed from parent to child—the first choice echoed forward through time.

Not as a warning.

Not as a mistake.

But as a gift.

The gift of knowledge. Of mortality. Of meaning.

The gift of being fully, completely, terrifyingly, beautifully human.

And it was enough.

It was everything.

It was the beginning of all things that truly mattered.

About The Author

Regina is a multi-genre author residing in the Hudson Valley region of New York. Before writing full-time, she worked as a fundraiser at a global environmental conservation organization. She loves the outdoors, animals, cooking, coffee, and spending her free time with her kids and pets.

Social Media – Get in Touch @ReginaBergenAuthor

Email: ReginaBergenAuthor@ReginaBergen.com

Website: www.ReginaBergen.com

Other Books

Be sure to check out these other books by Regina Bergen:

Poetry: Amidst Fading Blooms; Secrets Unearthed, Petals Unfurled; The Venom and The Rose; Of Weeping & Wildflowers; Between the Roots and the Roses

Rom-Com:

Pineberry Peak Novella Series: Faking It on the Slopes of Pineberry Peak – A Holiday Novella; Making It on the Slopes of Pineberry Peak – A Valentine's Day Novella

The Small Town Dirt Series: Dirty Hoe – A Gardening Romance; Dirty Latte – A Coffee Shop Romance; Dirty Laundry – A Laundromat/Dog Wash Romance

Middle-Grade Fiction: Paisley, Untethered; Paisley, Protector

Non-Fiction: But, He Was 6'2"

www.ingramcontent.com/pod-product-compliance
Lightning Source LLC
LaVergne TN
LVHW010541100826
845148LV00001B/262

* 9 7 8 1 6 4 9 2 3 1 1 3 0 *